About the Author

Tsitsi Tsopotsa started writing *Babel* during her MA in creative writing at Kingston University. She is working on her third novel as part of her PhD thesis at Middlesex University. The politics of marginalisation and voices of the underrepresented are key themes in her work. Tsitsi currently lives in England.

Babel

Tsitsi Tsopotsa

Babel

Vanguard Press

VANGUARD PAPERBACK

© Copyright 2024
Tsitsi Tsopotsa

A CIP catalogue record for this title is
available from the British Library.

ISBN 978 1 80016 803 9

Vanguard Press is an imprint of
Pegasus Elliot Mackenzie Publishers Ltd.
www.pegasuspublishers.com

First Published in 2024

Vanguard Press
Sheraton House Castle Park
Cambridge England

Printed & Bound in Great Britain

In memory of the lives of the seventy-two we lost in the Grenfell Fire. To my dad who instilled in me the value of books and that once started they should be finished (writing or reading), and my mum who taught me the nature of difference.

PABLO
23 MAY

The rain had started again. This time, a constant drizzle, enough to keep the ground wet. Pablo struck the pavement with a more determined stride. His shift at Elixir had ended at six p.m. He hoped to be home by seven that evening. He was relieved to see the familiar light illuminating the Mags & Fags Newsagent to his right. Darting through the thinning traffic, he stepped onto the pavement and pushed his way into the shop. The bell rang as Pablo crossed the threshold. As he passed the shelves, he nodded a greeting at Obi and Priyanuj, his neighbours, as they made their fizzy drink and snack selections. He settled on a bottle of Rioja, and then, took his place at the end of a short queue. A small screen, barely visible behind Sanjay, blinked out an episode of Breaking Bad. The back and forth at the counter replaced the muted sound.

A short English guy was trying to assert himself during his purchase of a pack of lagers.

"Listen, mate, I paid seven quid for it yesterday, today you're charging me eight. What you trying to do here?"

Sanjay, the shopkeeper's voice retained its even pitch. "It was never seven pounds yesterday. I'm telling you it was always eight pounds."

"I'll pay seven pounds," the young man said in a louder voice.

Pablo pushed his way to the front of the queue. He was at least a foot taller than the troublemaker.

"Everything all right, Sanjay?"

"I'm okay."

"Even if he's not okay. What you going to do about it?"

"Listen, either pay the £8 or get out." Pablo faced the man.

"You and whose army are going to get me out? Bloody foreigners. Think you can take me on?"

"Do I look like I need a fucking army?" said Pablo, through gritted teeth. "I've had a long day dealing with your types. Now either pay the man his eight pounds or get out."

"Yeah? You gonna make me? Eh?" The man pushed his face into Pablo's, trying to look menacing. Then he made the mistake of poking Pablo in the chest.

Pablo placed the wine on the counter and grabbed the man's collar, raising him off the ground.

"Now, watch me." He moved towards the door, frog-marching him to it. Priyanuj rushed past to hold the door open. Pablo dropped him, then pushed him out of the door, onto the pavement.

"Stay out, stupid fuck," Pryanaj shouted.

The young man got up off the ground, his jeans wet and grimy. He stared back with a sneer taking in their faces.

"Laters. I'll see yous around."

The bell rang as the door closed and a spontaneous cheer and applause rang around the shop.

"Thank you, Pablo. I don't think that he'll be back. Please help yourself." Sanjay indicated the abandoned pack of beers on the counter. Pablo waved them off.

"Maybe contribute them to the street party in August," Pablo suggested.

"You go next," Obi indicated to Pablo, stepping aside with his loaf of bread.

"Thanks. I'll have my usual rollups, please, Sanjay."

Back in the rain again, he checked the street to make sure the guy wasn't waiting for him outside. He noticed a small frame across the road, he could just make out the dark hair in the lights of the passing cars, the man was definitely facing him from across the road.

"I love this bloody country. Wouldn't change it for the world," Pablo said out loud.

He bent his head against the rain, looking up occasionally to judge the distance home. Ten minutes later, the building was within view but so was his neighbour, from the ground floor. Luke was undoubtedly looking for someone to sponge a cigarette or a few pounds off.

And then Pablo noticed the lone figure from before. He seemed to be facing him. He thought nothing of it. This guy wore a long coat, whereas the troublemaker from the shop wore a hoody. He focused on getting indoors without attracting Luke's attention, waiting in the shadows for Luke to go a little way down the street in the opposite direction. He saw his chance and sprinted to the front door, punched his way into the foyer and took the stairs two at a time, to the seventh floor. He tried the door; it was locked.

"Damn," he muttered under his breath. Cecilia wasn't home. "Where's the bloody key? I hope Abi doesn't hear me going in."

As he stood fumbling for his keys in his pocket, the door across the corridor creaked ajar, and a pair of brown eyes, on the same level as his shoulders, peered at him.

"Good evening, Abi."

"Hello, Pablo, how are you, my brother?"

"I'm good thanks. How about you?"

"I'm not good. How can I be good with that… " she indicated the far end of the corridor with her chin.

"What?"

"Did you see what that evil woman did to my front door?"

"What happened now?" He said, not making eye contact with her.

"You can't see it? Look, look… " she said, indicating the doormat. "You have to throw away that mat. I can't touch it. I can't even come out. Something bad will happen to me."

"I can't see anything."

"Look, look there. I saw it with my own two eyes. She came and dropped something, something here."

"I can't… "

"Just throw it. Nothing can happen to you, that thing is for me alone. She wants me dead." Her voice rose, and her eyes bulged at the effort.

Pablo stooped down grabbed the mat by the corner, and walked to the far end of the corridor until he reached number seventy-seven. He exchanged it for the mat there and brought that one back to Abi.

"No, no, you can't leave it here. I'll get her bad spirits. Throw it."

He dropped it instead into the black bin bag proffered by Abi and, after it had journeyed down the rubbish chute and the cover had clanged shut, he turned back to Abi. She was walking around her doorway sprinkling oil from a bottle.

"Father, son, holy spirit, heh, protect this my home, heh."

Pablo retrieved his key, while making his way back to his front door, the door at number seventy-seven flew open. The light from the window at the far end of the corridor was blocked out by a large black woman — her orange and purple kaftan a carnival tent.

"Ah ah, she's doing that juju… " Beauty shouted, her deep voice resonating down the corridor. "West African muti." She kissed her teeth. The carnival tent moved forward.

Pablo sighed to himself. *Not this again. I can't take another fight. But if I don't stop this now someone will feel obliged to call the police. Then the whole affair will drag on all night.*

"Beauty, please calm down. She's not doing anything to you. She's on her own doorstep."

"I'm just blessing my own door, eh. It's allowed." Abi shouted back.

"Are you a priest or a pastor now? How can you bless anything? It's juju. Now, how am I supposed to walk past there? Pabi?"

"My name's Pablo. If I can walk past here so can you. Look, watch me." Pablo walked past Abi's door a couple of times to demonstrate.

"If she's not doing anything to me, then she has nothing to fear," Abi shouted.

Another door opened. Betty stood in the doorway of number seventy-five, her legs bandaged up to her knees. The once-white bandages tinted to a dirty yellow by a smelly discharge.

"What's all that racket? I can't hear my bleeding telly with all that shouting. Is it those coloured ones again?" Betty addressed Pablo.

"Ah, ah, who are you calling coloured?" Beauty advanced further.

"Don't mind her — she's too old," Abi said. "We cannot fight her, wo. Hello, Betty, it's okay. Did the nurse forget to come again today?"

Abi hadn't wanted to fight Beauty again. The last fight had landed her in the accident and emergency department, nursing a fat lip and cuts and bruising to her face.

"My legs is wet. Everything is wet. They never come when they're supposed to,." Betty moaned.

"Let's go back inside. I'll make you a cup of tea. There'll be no more shouting out here." Pablo looked at the two women in the corridor. He went in with the old lady, glad to escape the drama.

"A nice civilised cup of tea." Betty shuffled back into her flat.

Pablo closed the door behind them and made his way to the kitchen while Betty continued to the front room to where one of Miss Marple's Mysteries was unravelling. The kitchen was always in the same state with dust accumulating on the cooker. He doubted that she ever ate. He opened the kitchen window and stood as near to it as possible to get the stench of urine out. He wondered who he should call to look into it.

"No sugar? he asked over the volume of the television.

"That's right. And a couple of biscuits. They're in the tin on the left. The red and blue one."

"What did you have for tea, Betty?"

"Oh, umm — I can't remember that far back."

"Shall I make you a sandwich instead?"

"Oh! That would be nice. A cheese one. That would be nice."

"Here you go." Pablo left her with the cheese sandwich and a fresh cup of tea. As an afterthought, he had put two biscuits on the tray.

"Oh, you're ever such a good boy, Pablo. Cecilia is lucky to have you. You go on now. You don't want to keep her waiting."

"I'll lock the door and slip the key through the letterbox."

The corridor was empty. Both doors of the warring parties were shut. Pablo found his keys and wearily let himself into his flat. He made his way to the kitchen and uncorked the bottle of wine. Five minutes later, he was out on the balcony, lighting a freshly-rolled cigarette. He shielded himself from the rain and stared at the light from the street lamps' spotlighted raindrops as they raced downwards as if flowing through a giant sieve. This was his idea of sexy weather, with Cecilia damp and her hair in a mess. Her distinct scent evoked memories of rain and sex. When she looked like that, she reminded him of Jorge Amado's Gabriela in Gabriela, Clove, and Cinnamon, which he'd read years ago. He wasn't one for romance novels, but he'd found it in the library and started to read it because he was curious about the lesser-known parts of Brazil. The book was set in the 1920s in a little town called Ilheus and a challenging romance between Nicab and Gabriela, Pablo fell in love with Gabriela and her environment. Ever since then, he'd been looking for his own Gabriela and had found her in Cecilia. Her large nose drew attention to almond-shaped hazel eyes. He outlined his lips with his forefinger as he yearned for her full, soft lips on his. Sexy seemed a more fitting word to describe her than beautiful or pretty. He liked to get his fingers caught in her thick mane of dark chocolate hair, its sandalwood scent lingered on the pillows. Then he thought about her slim body, the way her hips broadened out and accentuated her waist. He pictured his hands tracing the curves of her breasts…

He lingered a little while longer in the damp air desiring her and after he'd finished his second glass of wine, he turned into the small flat to prepare the evening meal.

Cecilia arrived home an hour later to find a dinner of tuna pasta and salad on the table. Pablo turned the lights off and lit two candles. She smiled as she watched Pablo shovelling forkfuls of pasta, tuna, and salad greens into his mouth.

When he paused for a sip of wine, she teased him. "Are you planning on seducing me tonight?"

"Of course, but we need nourishment. No?"

Cecilia smiled.

"What did you eat today?" she asked. Her yardstick of how well his day had gone.

"I just had a sandwich — tuna." He washed the thought down with a large gulp of wine. "This is good wine. Sanjay is starting to stock the better stuff."

"And tuna again? For supper? Interesting choice, is your imagination starting to flail?"

"Not at all. I just had more of a taste for it. Hope you didn't also have tuna for lunch?"

"Have you noticed how our English has improved, ever since we started to speak in English? Wouldn't it be great if you improved your Portuguese enough to impress my family?"

"It must be all the role play we do every weekend. Last weekend it was Spanish."

"It gets a little confusing sometimes — maybe we should stick to one book, one language — Portuguese."

"When will you polish up your Spanish then?"

"When we get through the next book." She phrased it like a question, but Pablo knew that she had made up her mind and it was easier to go with it so that he could get on with what she had planned for the rest of the evening.

"So, Brazilian weekend starting from tomorrow?"

"Yes, what about a theme from Gabriela, Clove, and Cinnamon?"

"Mmm… You must have read my mind. Earlier today, I was thinking about how much you remind me of Gabriela."

She put her glass down, and moved her chair back allowing her dressing gown to gape open.

"Any particular scene you want to play out?" she said, her hands on her hips.

"What about the journey from the interior… you know, those nights out in the open."

"I don't remember any sex scenes there."

"No, Jorge left that up to the reader's imagination. He was after all writing in the early twentieth century."

"Well, my imagination works fine."

The next morning, everything outside looked wet and murky. A ray of weak sunshine turned the pavements into mirrored, slippery surfaces. The traffic and a few early shoppers roused the streets. Cecilia had chosen a maxi-length dress with large blood-red orchids on a green background. A red carnation in her long, black, wavy hair secured it to one side so that it draped over her right shoulder. She indicated a lone fox with her parasol as Pablo moved towards her. She was a foot shorter than Pablo which brought his green bowtie to just above her eye-line. She grinned and turned away. Pablo noticed.

"What?" He asked, his hands running over his white linen suit.

"Nothing." She looked up at him again, flashing her dimples as she tried to hide her smile.

"You're laughing at my bowtie? Don't you want me? Is it because I'm flawed?" he joked, indicating his bowtie.

"You must wear what you want; it's your body."

"I want to make you proud."

"No, no! Nicab doesn't say that."

"But does Nicab do this?" He said stepping closer to her and pulling her towards him. She giggled. He closed his eyes, inhaling her scent.

"Yes, but remember it was in the dark. They had to hide from Gabriela's uncle." Cecilia brought the book out so they could check who was right.

"I don't care. I want to declare my love publicly. Madam…" he addressed the elderly woman coming towards them.

"Bugger off!" the woman replied. "All that kissing so early in the morning. Disgusting."

Cecilia snickered and pulled Pablo back before he could offend the lady any further. He noticed Beauty's face at the window above, in their building.

"Those women are going to kill each other," he said, still looking up.

"Portuguese, please, voce quer dizer Abi and Beauty?" Cecilia asked.

"I don't understand it."

"It's a man thing. Abi claims that Beauty stole her man. Or is trying to. It's best to stay out of it. I don't know why you think you have to referee it all the time."

"I can't stay out of it. I keep getting dragged into their fights," Pablo said, eyeing a character across the street. It was the trouble-maker from the previous night.

Another argument had broken out between him and Pryanuj. Two shady-looking characters appeared from behind the small guy and were circling Pryanuj.

"Pryanuj needs my help," said Pablo, and he threw the book towards Cecilia.

"Pablo, no!"

But Pablo had already run into the road. He ignored the hooting cars of annoyed drivers, as he dodged their bonnets.

"What's up?" he said to Pryanuj under his breath.

"It's that little shitster, from last night. Brought his mates."

"Three of us versus two of you. You're not so clever now, are you?" the runt said, indicating his friends on Pryanuj's right.

One of the friends stepped closer and swung at Pryanuj, aiming for the right side of his jaw. He felt the force of the wind behind that punch, which he blocked by forcing his wrist against the attacker's. Another fist was aimed at Pablo's head. Pablo was unable to block it in time. He only managed to step back. The blow landed on his chest. He was temporarily winded. He took another step back then one large one forward, getting a fist to the guy's stomach, with his full weight behind it.

"Ugh!" the guy spat, followed by a fit of coughing.

While he was doubled over, Pablo stepped in and kneed the man, hard in the face. Blood sprayed on his trousers, a pretty pattern of even-sized dots. He winced in agony. When he fell to the ground, Pablo kicked him in the back.

"Ahhh!" the guy screamed.

He lay there for a few minutes, the pavement around his head turning bright red.

"Fuck, you broke my nose."

"You came for a fight. you got a fight." Pablo pulled back his leg as if to kick him again. The guy covered his head with both hands and squeezed into a foetal position. Pablo turned to Pryanuj. The cars had slowed down to take in the fight. One or two shouts of encouragement emerged from their windows

Meanwhile, Pryanuj had thrown the smaller bloke with a judo move. A dull thud was audible as he hit the concrete. He lay facing upwards. Pryanuj moved on to the remaining guy. He looked uncertain now that his crew was out of action. He hesitated. Pryanuj stepped up to him. The man raised his hands.

"I don't want to fight you. I'm just going to leave. Okay?"

Pryanuj turned to Paolo as they heard the sound of approaching police sirens, and said, "Let's go."

Pryanuj went back to the shop and Pablo scoured the small crowd that had gathered across the road for Cecilia, but she had left. He went up the street to the café that she liked. Au Lait was almost full. A few familiar faces smiled up at him in recognition. There was a buzz of good-humoured conversation. Roasting coffee beans punctured the air with their pungent aroma. Pablo found Cecilia sitting at a table for two in the window. She refused to make eye contact with him.

"So, you feel like a man? Fighting in the streets like a criminal."

"I had to help Pryanuj out. He's our neighbour and friend."

"You just thought that... oh my God, look at your hands! You've hurt yourself."

"It's nothing."

"No, we must go home you need to wash those cuts. If you get any germs in them, they may get infected."

"There's no need"

"We go now — come." She took a final gulp of her cappuccino and set her cup down loudly on the table. When Pablo still did not move, she pushed her chair back and glared at him. Pablo stood and followed her out.

The crowd had dispersed, and the few people left over stood in twos and threes describing the fight. Pablo grinned at the exaggerated accounts he overheard on the way back to their flat. The earlier animated chatter was reduced to a few words in the lift. Cecilia led the way to the bathroom and handed Pablo a bottle of Dettol for his bruised hands. He stood by the window after he'd washed. The three men had left before the police arrived. He observed the two police officers give up on their enquiries and after circling the area in their vehicle, he saw them drive off.

When he felt that it was safe to leave, a little after two p.m., he and Cecilia headed out. This time the sun was hot, so they opted to look for somewhere to have a beer. Music blared from a window in their building. It was one of the neighbours that they barely knew. Luke sat outside in a vest and jean shorts. Much to Pablo's annoyance, he was obliged to give him one of his pre-rolled cigarettes. The sickly, sweet tune of the ice cream van rang out, as it turned onto the street, Cecilia waved it down.

"We have to walk a bit. You know — in keeping with the book," she said as she handed him a cone. "I thought we might have a picnic in the park before the sun goes down. Then you can woo me the way Nicab wooed Gabriela."

"Park? When it was so wet earlier?"

"The sun's starting to dry the ground — maybe it'll be all right."

"Or maybe we can drop into Bernie's and sit in the beer garden?" Cecilia nodded.

"I know how you'll get more practice. Nicab used to tell Gabriela about his ambitions. You can tell me about yours."

"I hope I have the right vocabulary." Pablo looped his arm through hers and they sauntered towards the commercial area. "As much as I hate working at Elixir, I'll have to stay there for another year after I finish university. I need to save up some money. I want to move back to Spain to open a web design and digital marketing company. My customers will be those small producers in the countryside. You know; designers, artists and maybe even the smaller fisheries. No one is doing it at the moment, so there's an opportunity to make good money. I want you to come with me."

"I have to go where I can get a permit."

"Are you just sticking to the plot in the book? Or do you mean that?"

"I have to be practical. How would we live? If you are just starting up, then you'll need support. I won't get a job as a project manager in Spain. So maybe I'd have to opt for a job where I can't use my qualifications. Besides, two years is a long way away, perhaps we can discuss it later. This Brexit thing — I might need to leave anyway." They dodged a young man running to catch the number three bus.

"Oh God! This relationship is cursed like Nicab and Gabriela's. I should have chosen another book."

"Pablo, don't be so dramatic. Please!"

"This is serious. I find the woman of my dreams. Then she tells me she has no plans to be with me in two years."

"That's not what I said. I love you, Pablo. We will try and look at some jobs nearer the time."

"Okay. Okay."

LUKE
25 MAY

You step away from the front door of the flats. Less than a minute later, you hear the door slam as someone slips past you. It's then that you remember you've lost your keys. Maybe the lady in flat seventy-three will let you in again without asking too many questions.

Shit! I'm down to my last fag.

You search the dark pavement for any movement. Some guy is making his way towards you. Since you're not sure of your chances with this stranger, you turn back to face the direction that you were walking in. You cup your hands over the cigarette-butt to shelter it against the rain, trying to light it for the fifth time. The lighter spits out a short orange tongue; it's immediately drowned by a raindrop.

"That's no fuckin' use."

You fling the lighter onto the pavement in disgust. It bounces into the road and is rushed down the drain by the rain.

"Need a light?"

The voice disturbs you. A man produces a lighter which he helps you to shield. You eye him in the flickering light, wondering what else he's good for.

"Cheers, mate!"

"Live around here?" he asks, he sounds like he's local.

You direct a spiral of smoke at the building you've just left.

"Off to the pub then?"

He's giving you the once over, taking in your knackered trainers, your faded jeans.

You take the opportunity to check him out in more detail. His dark hair has been glued down by the rain. You recognise the pink and black check of Burberry beneath his jacket. His trainers mirror the check on their beige background.

"Just calculating the funds."

"Maybe, I can see my way to buying you a pint. That's if you can show us the way to the pub."

"You want to buy me a pint? Why?"

"I'm new around here — just — I haven't got my bearings... I need someone to... tell me about this place."

"Yeah? Why's that then?"

"Like I said, I just moved to the area."

There's a flash of irritation in his manner.

"Right."

Your curiosity and force of habit propel you onwards. You cross the road leading him into the open door of the Devil's Punchbowl.

You can't remember the last time you were able to pay for a round. Not that you have any mates to go down the pub with, but... The guy is delayed while he inches closer to a mini-skirted blonde woman. He stares at her until she turns. They make eye contact. You think that you can make out a bloke by his chat-up line, so you move forward to stand just behind him.

"All right, darlin'?" he asks her.

"You talking to me?" She sounds a bit tetchy as she looks down at him. Her nose is turned up at the end.

"Who else?" He of the Burberry mix-and-match moves closer to the woman. He looks towards you and mouths something that you cannot make out. But you imagine he's said something like 'she's a slice short of a loaf.' You smile at him, encouraging him to make a fool of himself — the girl is clearly out of his league.

"Naff off! Yeah?" She elbows him out of the way to be next at the bar.

You watch as he clears out a nostril onto his hand and wipes it on the hair hanging on her arm away furthest away from him. She turns to her right to check who has touched her. The two of you are on her left. As you leave, he says loud enough for her to hear.

"Did you see her? What a chav!"

"D'you know her?"

"Got off with her last time, didn't I?"

The girl walks up to the two of you, opens her mouth to say something but decides instead to give him the finger and walks off.

"Same to you, sweetheart,." Andy shouts after her.

You're not really interested, just in the pint. Then you'll do one.

You follow him to the back of the pub where he finds a table. You eye the amber liquid begging to be drunk. You look for any traces of snot. He raises a glass so you grab the other.

"Cheers, mate, — Luke." It burns cold down your throat and you don't stop till half the glass is gone.

"Andy — so how long have you lived around here? Are they all minging like that one?" His head indicates the blonde who has rejoined her friends a few tables away.

"Going on two years now."

"In the same block?"

"Yeah."

You wriggle in your seat hoping you won't have to dredge up the past and how you got to live there — and how the state and your mother are permanent features in your life.

"I suppose you know everyone in the block by now?"

"Most, not all — why do you ask?"

"I met a couple of them the other night. I just wondered — that's all."

During the second round you try to find out a bit more about him — nothing's adding up.

"Was you in a fight?" You ask the bruising on his face looks fresh.

"Bloody foreigners jumped me, didn't they? There was four of them to one of me. Wish I could say 'you should have seen the other guy.' But it wasn't a fair fight."

You know that there are a number of 'foreigners' in your block and you wonder if this is the reason for Andy's interest. You fall silent and let Andy do the talking.

He talks about how much money he's made in the last month. He doesn't say how and you don't ask. You think you'll give him the slip after the next pint. You've reached your capacity and he's getting boring.

"I'm out of funds," Andy says, when you come back from taking a slash.

"I'll get you next time." You know that's highly unlikely, but you want to show willing.

"Nah, you're all right."

You shrug your coat on and lead the way to the door. Andy wastes time with his coat and doesn't leave with you.

The rain has stopped but the air feels damp. The pedestrians have emptied into the terraced houses. A few lights beam from the windows before blinking out. You stare at the hazy lights of cars as they rush towards you, then spray you as they hurtle on into the darkness.

You arrive at your block of flats, fumble around in your pockets then swear softly when you can't find the keys. Then you remember misplacing them and press a few random flat numbers including seventy-three until one of them buzzes you in without enquiring who it is.

You stumble into the foyer — you can't wait to get in and you forget to check that the door has secured itself after you. You wonder how you're going to get the lock changed as you can't keep leaving your flat unlocked. As you walk into your flat and turn to close your door behind you, Andy shouts out,

"Be seeing you, mate!"

Fuckin' weirdo.

The remainder of a tin of beans and two pieces of toast is your supper which you eat standing in the kitchen supervised by the bare bulb overhead. You remember the home-cooked dinners you used to have when you were working, but that was then, and now you force the beans down with a wash of tea. You contribute your empty plate to the pile of dirty dishes in the sink.

The next morning, after a rare shower, you're dressed in your last clean shirt. You use a drop of hair gel to emphasise the parting in your hair. You wish you could afford another pair of sneakers or at least clean the years off the ones you're wearing.

The blinding sun forces you to use your hand to shield the cash point screen, which assures you that your benefits are available for use. You immediately withdraw thirty pounds. Next stop, the local Tescott Superstore, where you wander the aisles displaying toys and little girl's dresses. You finger a few of them but the price tags put you off. You realise that you can either do lunch or a present and definitely a couple of bottles of cider with either choice. Tough decision but you know that MacD's is always a big hit.

As an afterthought, you get a giant-sized birthday card from Cards Galore and write it out in a corner shop where you borrow a pen from the lottery stand.

Darling Charlotte, Happy Birthday. Love Daddy

You scribble her name in giant letters on the envelope. You arrive at the bus stop just in time to catch the ten-thirty bus.

The number seventy-three bus slowly fills as it nears Shepherd's Bush. You stare ahead, nervous about meeting her. At the last stop, you slither down the steps and out into the sunshine. You take your time to cross the green, and perch on a bench to face the big black gates across the road. Beyond the gate, you read the big bold letters Babes n' Tots Alphabet Centre.

You've read it for the tenth time and wonder how many tots have mastered the alphabet, when a V reg Clio draws up.

Fuck me!

You watch the blonde squeeze herself out from behind the wheel. Her thighs and stomach rebel against the waistband of the white cropped jeans. She's wearing a floaty, pink thing that sits across her shoulders and chest. She lights a cigarette and smokes it with her right hand while the fingers of her left jab at her phone.

The other mothers haven't arrived yet. You wonder whether this is the best time to approach her. You anticipate an unpleasant scene scarring a perfect day, fouling the still air and your mind's picture of the picnic green for happy families.

You keep an eye on the blonde across the road. When she smiles at her screen, you feel that it's safe to approach her.

"Hello Mel."

"What the fuck you doing here?"

"It's Charlotte's birthday, isn't it? I'm taking her to MacD's innit."

"You can't just rock up and take her. I have plans for her birthday."

"I can wait and take her afterwards."

"Well, she'll be tired."

The clouds smothered the sun and a light breeze on the back of your neck make you wonder if you should have brought your denim jacket for later.

"You can't stop me from seeing my own daughter. After all, I am paying maintenance."

Mel goes back to her car and makes a show of locking the doors.

"Where d'you get the car from?"

"Bought it, didn't I."

"Where did you get the money from?"

"When you work — you get money."

You wonder if she is seeing someone. You think about asking her, but the other mothers turn up at the gate. Then the children come through the gates, hand-in-hand, shouting goodbye to their teachers and each other.

"Charlotte! It's daddy, it's daddy! Happy birthday darlin'!"

She steps forward shyly, sneaking looks at her mother. You sweep her upwards, hug her tightly and kiss her forehead.

"Happy birthday, darlin' — how about MacD's to celebrate your birthday?"

She nods her head happily, her index finger pressing her teeth and her eyes looking up at you from beneath her lashes.

"I never agreed to that, did I?" Mel tries to kill the vibe.

"Oh! Com'on, it's not like I see her everyday, you can come too."

She looks at Charlotte smiling up at you and responds by unlocking the car. The short drive to the nearest MacDonald's is filled with excited chatter from Charlotte in the back seat. When you tried to sit with your daughter, Mel had done one.

"I'm not the bloody chauffeur, am I?"

When you're strapped into the passenger seat, she drills you — how comes you're off in the middle of the week? When are you going to pay more maintenance? Blah blah. And you feel like asking her when she's going to stop doing your head in.

Mel wanders around the restaurant searching for a table. You and Charlotte choose the meals and find Mel at a four-seater table. When the last of the chips are eaten, Mel starts to jab her straw in her sprite-flavoured ice cubes. You try to engage Charlotte, delaying the inevitable.

"Is that it?" Mel's eyes pierce yours. "No present?"

"That's all I could afford."

"So, what's the point? You should have just bought a present."

"Well, at least I got to see her. And spend some time with her."

"Then she won't see you till her next birthday. Not much of a dad, are you?"

"I'd see her more often if I could."

"You've seen her now so scram! Go on scram! Back to the little hole you crawled out of. Nothing but scum."

"'Bye then, darlin'. Daddy will be back as soon as I can. All right, my princess?"

Charlotte nods sadly. She watches her mother's mouth. Charlotte doesn't stand up and hug you, she just concentrates on the last of her banana milkshake.

You take the rejection on the chin, satisfied that at least an hour or so is better than none at all. You try to think about new ways of getting a job, that will improve your status with Mel. Hopefully, Charlotte will soon be able to come and visit. On the way home, you stop in Fags & Mags.

"I'll have that bottle, and this cider."

"You mean the vodka — small or big?" Sanjay asks, before putting them on the counter. It's nearly five o'clock and you're keen to avoid the workers. Especially those from your building. You hurriedly stuff the bottles into the blue plastic bag offered by Sanjay as you hear the bell ring in another customer.

You enter the building and flat without attracting attention from any of the neighbours. The streets are starting to fill up with leisurely commuters. The weather is good, and no one seems to be in a hurry any more.

As you walk into the kitchen, you think that you hear a voice at the front door.

"You okay, mate? Just thought I'd drop by."

"Er… how?" You remember that last time you hadn't checked the street door had shut behind you, this time he could have used the same strategy you used to get in. You're worried he's going to keep coming back.

"You should check the door behind you when you come in. I just happened to be passing and I saw you. I see you've got a stash there. Planning on sharing?"

You invite Andy to sit down. It's the least you can do after he financed the previous night's beverages. You run two glasses under the cold tap and place the two bottles on the small kitchen table.

"Nah, nah, give that a proper wash. I can still see something stuck at the bottom."

You produce another glass from the cupboard as you haven't replaced the washing-up liquid, amongst other things. Andy looks around your flat. You sit opposite him and pour a generous shot of vodka into each glass then pour more cider into the pint glasses that you pinched from the pub. A few minutes later, you repeat the round.

"Steady, mate."

Andy doesn't drink his vodka immediately.

"So, to what do I owe a visit?"

"Do I need a reason?"

"You don't need a reason, but I'm guessing you're a busy man."

"That I am. I've got my fingers in a lot of pies."

"Know anywhere I can get a job?"

"Err, what kind of job?"

"I used to work as an administrator."

"Yeah?"

"I did quite well at school... "

"What happened then? Why didn't you learn a trade or something?"

"I did, well sort of — the school arranged an apprenticeship in project management for a construction company."

"How long were you there for?"

"Six months."

"That's not... "

"I know — the company folded up. They had promised to promote me — co-ordinator and pay for my project management course. But it all went up in smoke."

You down a third shot of vodka and regret blurting out all of that hard luck stuff.

"How long ago was that?" Andy sniffs, you watch his eyes roam the walls and rest on a small black patch peeping from behind the television.

"About two years ago."

"Are you sure you still have those skills? I mean it's been a while — a year, two?"

You think that Andy is a few years older and might know about these things.

"I'll take anything."

"What made you think about it now? I mean you've been out of work for two years."

You get thrown off a bit as you see Andy wrinkle his nose and adjust the thin, faded cotton curtains, flinging the window wide open. Warm but slightly fresher air surges in.

"It's my little girl… "

You fall silent and watch the curtains shift with the wind. The dying evening sun makes you think of endings. Perhaps it's time you stopped hoping for a job and looked at some other options. The problem is what — perhaps Andy… ? The shouts and laughter of the children on the green filter in with the sounds of the traffic and bring you back into the room and the discomfort that Andy's questions are causing.

"You were saying… "

"I want to see my daughter more often. You know — get her things and that."

"Yeah, I know what it's like. I have two of my own."

"She lives with her mother. If I don't have funds… "

"How comes you're — you know… "

"Just before I got made redundant, she fell pregnant with Charlotte. Then we moved in with her mother. After Charlotte was born, I couldn't stay there no more."

"What if I could get you a small job? I mean you're not exactly — I don't mean to be rude and that — but you're not exactly living in a palace... "

"Anything." You sit upright and pour the contents of your glass down your throat.

"It'll just be running errands and that — interested?"

"Yeah — cash?"

"Of course. It won't be every day. Just now and then. We'll pay you fifty quid per job."

If I can get three jobs per week at least plus my benefits — about two hundred and thirty pounds a week.

"You got a mobile?"

"Yeah, but there's no airtime, you know."

"Give me... " Andy sits poised with his phone waiting to enter the digits. "It's Luke, isn't it?"

He produces a twenty-pound note which he places next to the glasses. You decide to ignore it, then he catches you looking at it so you ask, as nonchalantly as you can.

"What's that for?"

"Just a little goodwill. Laters!"

Alone again, you toast your good fortune with another round of drinks.

BETTY
JUNE

I like to feel the sun against the closed windows. The boiler's set to the timer so, even in summer, it's on. I have to wait until my Angela comes to change it. She's ever such a good girl. If I turn it off, I might not know how to turn it back on again in the winter. Besides, I like to hear it go on at seven in the morning. It's reassuring. I'll get up now and wash my face.

Oh! The bed's wet again. I'll have to put the sheets in the wash. Thing is, I can't pull 'em off. Haven't the strength in my arms. It gets cold sitting in that chair all day long. Where's my pink cardie? The one my Harry bought me when we went to Blackpool for a weekend. All them years ago. It reminds me of candyfloss. We had a good summer that year. Love. Laughter. Good company. My Harry was always good for a laugh.

I can't believe that's me in the mirror. Those ugly pink puffs beneath my eyes. I used to be able to deflate them with a hot towel, but they hardly budge now. Still, the wrinkles don't look so bad this morning — a little face cream will fill them out a bit. There, that's better. That toasted almond lipstick's a real treat. These days, all they go on about is bright white teeth. Who's goin' see my mine now? Them all sticking out like that at the bottom. Put more lippy on that's what'll do, cover the red mark that my teeth left. I'm always biting them in my sleep.

At least I still have my hair. I like the way it shimmers in the bedroom light. I'll just give it a quick brush. Smooth it all down again. There, that'll do. Wonder if anyone's coming 'round today.

There, if I fold back the duvet a bit like that. I can air the bed out — open them windows. If someone comes, they can just take the sheet out for me.

I'll just go over to the kitchen and see about breakfast.

That little walk from the bedroom makes me so out of breath. I know it's just a short distance, but I can hardly breathe when I get here.

I'll just stand here for a minute till it comes back — not long now.

There's last night's leftovers — those bloody microwave dinners — I can't stand them. Not fit for dogs. I'll just chuck it. If I run the hot tap over them mugs and that from yesterday — there. I'll just fill the kettle and I think I'll have a slice of toast and marmalade. Oh! the bread's mouldy must be the heat in here. I wonder if that nice boy — what's his name? — is ever coming back. I could ask him to get me a few things. Cornflakes it is — I'll just take them through. Lorraine will be on in a minute.

Oh, bloody hell, that's done it. Them bleeding bandages almost tripped me up. Now, the tea's left more brown stains on top of the old ones in the carpet.

Remember when this was new? I could do with a new carpet, maybe change the curtains. I'm tired of looking at it all. I could get another maroon carpet and maybe some grey curtains this time. Velvet ones. But who's gonna do all that? I need to get to that Carpetrite place. How am I going to do that? Get there? The chair's still all right even though the grandchildren disabled the massage function. That's when they still used to come 'round. Them and their mum have no time for me. Still, I can put my feet up and watch Lorraine.

Where's the remote?

That's right, Lorraine — you ask them.

My tea's lukewarm now — I'll just have to drink it.

Well done, Lorraine!

Shouldn't have drunk the tea — now I need to wee. By the time I manage to get up, Jeremy would have introduced the guests and that. I don't want to miss that. I'll go in the break.

What a stupid girl that is — the way she speaks to her mother. And the mother just puts up with it — in my day, none of that would happen. This is a good enough time to go to the lav. Maybe by the time I get back, she'd have remembered that she's her mother.

If the nurse doesn't come today, I'll cut off these bandages myself. If I just shuffle, I can be in the bathroom in a few minutes. Oh hell, the wee won't wait — I'll shuffle just a little faster. I'll just wait here a few minutes — get my breathing right. When I get back — I'll use my inhaler.

The nurse said, 'No more than two breaths.' She'd said in that condescending manner. Who does she think she's talking to like that? And it's my lungs so I'll bloody well take more breaths if I want to. Now, where's the bloody thing?... Three... four!

Oh, Doctors. Sometimes I get tired of the telly — like now. But what else can I do? Can't make my own clothes no more. If someone could just come round and thread the needle on the machine. Thing is...

Hang on...

Is that the intercom?

I must ask them to increase the volume on that — I can only just about hear it when I've got the telly on. Better hurry.

"Hello."

"Is that Mrs Lyons? It's the nurse. May I come in?"

I'll just buzz her in. Thank God I made it in time. That's it. She should be in by now. I'll try and make it back before she gets up here.

"Come in! It's open."

Not seen this blonde one before. If she'd just taken a little time to get dressed properly and lose a little weight, she'd be something to look at. Still, I suppose she doesn't need beauty to be a good nurse. Never knew blonde people could have brown eyes, and such tiny ones at that. Maybe she's a bottle blonde.

"You look a bit flushed, nurse — you all right?"

"Just get my breath back. Can we turn the tv off for a minute?" I nod. "That's better, now I can hear you."

Peppermint breath.

"Lift not working?"

"No, I always use the stairs. My name is Jo, I'm the respiratory nurse. I've come to see you about your COPD. May I call you Betty?"

"Oh! The breathing nurse. Yes, everyone calls me Betty. Mrs Lyons is too formal in your own living room. Find somewhere to sit."

The respiratory nurse out of breath?

"How have you been? We haven't seen you for at least three months. I was going to call, but I thought I'd pop 'round instead."

"I'm glad to see you — but I usually get my afro nurse. She's the one that looks after me."

I suppose she'll expect me to open my blouse and let the draft in. Oh God! That stethoscope is cold.

"And how are you coping with life in general? You look as though you could use some help with a few things."

"No, no, I don't need any carers. I can manage myself. My daughter takes care of all of that. I'm just waiting for her to call."

"When did you last speak to your daughter?"

Do they train them to snoop around your house like this? So, what if I haven't done my housework? I'm the one who has to live here. Should I tell her — it's none of your bleeding business. But I can't be rude. No one will come 'round if I give her what for.

"Before she went on 'oliday. She's ever such a good girl."

I know she asked me something else, but I can't remember what it was.

"What about a cup of tea?" Maybe she'll offer to make me one.

"I can't stop, but I can make you one, if you like?"
That's the one.

"No sugar!" She might even do a little washing up for me. I wonder whether to trouble her with my bed.

"Here you go. I'll call the district nurse to come and see you about your legs. I'd like to stop longer, but I have to see three more patients before lunchtime."

Maybe I'll ask the district nurse when she comes. This one seems a bit posh.

"Oh, but that was kind of you to drop in. Will the district nurse come today?"

"I'll ask them to come as soon as possible. 'Bye, Betty. It was nice to see you."

Well, at least I got a piping hot cup of tea out of her. Not very chatty though.

My Harry used to come home round about this time. We'd have soup and a roll together. Then we'd have a tumble in the bedroom. At about four o'clock he'd peel the potatoes or whatever and I'd come in and cook our tea. What's it all for? I mean you do all those things only to end up sitting in a chair all day long watching telly?

"OH HARRY, WHY'D YOU HAVE TO LEAVE ME? NOW I'M JUST WAITING TO DIE! ALL ON MY OWN."

I'm screaming now and throw the mug at the wall, making sure to miss the television. There's a crack as the cup hits the wall, it gulps and burps, next thing, there's splashes of warm brown liquid on the wall. Then the cup slides to the carpet in two halves that leave thick trails behind it. It lands on the rug with a small bounce. The stain looks like a shadow.

That's the loneliest moment.

Me and Harry's like those two halves of the cup. The messy life, and half-forgotten memories left trailing behind us. Except I'm still here remembering. On me own.

I fall into a deep sleep. Something wakes me up.

"Hello!" I shout towards the door. But no one answers. I scramble to the passage. My bladder's full again. What do I do first, toilet or intercom?

Inie meenie, mini mo — the intercom wins.

"Hello, hello… "

There is silence. I'm wishing 'mini mo' had landed on the toilet. I feel the warm liquid as it trickles down. The bandages will suck it up, so I won't have to worry about the floor. I hope they don't smell.

That's what you get for falling asleep. Stupid bitch.

"Bleeding people, won't bleeding wait."

I find myself in the bathroom with a pair of the nurse's scissors. I start with the pants. I flick them into the basin and sit down on the toilet seat wondering where to start.

I hear it — the faint tap tapping on the door. Before I can answer, someone tries the door handle. The bathroom door's open, soon as they step into that passage, they'll see me.

The indignity of it all. No bleeding respect.

"Who is it?" My voice sounds harsher than I'd intended but look at me.

"Hello, Betty, it's the district nurse. Hello."

"What do you want?" I ask this coloured face that looks like it's been cut clean from its body. She's smiling at me. Do I know her? Look at her, all skin and bone, looks like she ought to be on a feeding programme. Maybe she's from one of those countries that's always asking for money.

Right here, in my bleeding front room.

Her tunic and trousers hang loosely around her thin frame. When she smiles, her teeth seem to take up half of her face. Her hair's in shoulder-length braids or dreadlocks — whatever they call them. Quite neat I must say, styled in a bob! With a side parting! I wonder how she gets them to be so even.

"You haven't met me before, Betty. My name is Schola."

"Another new one. Why can't I get the same nurse?" It's disturbing all these new faces. "You'd better come in then, hadn't you?"

I wait for her to close the door. Then I start the painful trek. Trying to think of other things she can do for me whilst she's here. The ping pinging of pain shoots right up

47

my legs. I stop for a bit. But she's busy washing her hands in the bathroom, so doesn't notice. I throw myself into the chair and raise my legs up. I can't reconcile my broken flesh with my youth. I feel resentful of this nurse walking towards me. As she enters the room, the light catches the sharpness of her blue tunic and contrasts it against the pitch-black braided hair and shiny white teeth. It reminds me of what I can't be. Yet I'm starting to warm towards her and breathing comes easier.

"What did you say your name was?"

"Schola."

"What kind of a name is that?"

"Betty, I've come to do your legs." She's trying to be professional, but she sounds mean. "Do you have any supplies in the house?"

I point out a large plastic bag in the corner. She doesn't waste any time getting straight to work. She sticks my feet into a bowl of warm water. It feels nice.

She seems nice, anyway. I should be grateful that she came.

"Do you live alone, Betty?"

"My Harry left me ten years ago now."

"Oh, you must miss him. Is that your wedding day?" She points at the large, gilt-framed black and white photo on the wall above the mantle with her chin.

"I have such beautiful memories, but they make me so sad." I hold the tears back.

The lace curtain billows inwards then out on a slight breeze. I imagine it sucking all the memories out with it. I shiver as they pass over me. She's watching me closely, so I smile back.

"That's you all patched up. Have you had lunch?"

"It's not lunchtime yet."

"It's one-thirty in the afternoon, Betty. Why don't I make you a sandwich?"

"That's not your job. Don't worry yourself." I don't want her snooping around in my fridge. Maybe that lad, Palbo… Pablo, will drop in and offer to do some shopping.

"It'll only take me a minute." She goes into the kitchen before I can stop her. She produces an egg sandwich and a cup of tea.

"Who does your shopping, Betty?"

"My daughter. I expect she'll be in sometime today."

"Betty, we haven't been able to get hold of your daughter. We've left messages and she hasn't replied. I'm going to refer you to the social worker so that she can organise some help for you. Is that okay?"

"I don't need help. All those bleeding people nosing around my drawers."

"It won't be like that at all. Look, if I get the social worker, they'll just come for a chat and ask you before they do anything. Okay?" She grabs my hand and pats it. Wonder if she'd have liked me patting her head whilst she was doing my legs.

"I suppose if she's just coming to talk, then that's okay."

Hope she's nice.

I watch her eyes roam around the room again. They settle on the brown splash on the wall. It's dry now and looking more like a dirty patch. She says nothing and goes 'round and picks the pieces of the mug. I see her eyes take in the grey sofa against the wall by the door. it used to be grand when it was new, it contrasted nicely against the big red flowers on the wallpaper. Now it's covered in dust. Even the cushions look dull. She picks up one of the Television Guides that are weighing down the coffee table. She looks at me as if she wants to ask why I still need the ones from last year, then she decides against it. She walks over to the glass cabinet with mother's old tea set and all the tat that I inherited. I remember not wanting to part from them. Anything to hold on to her memory. I know she can see the dust, but I'm past caring.

Satisfied with her snooping skills, she turns and smiles at me. I don't like the pity in her eyes.

Then she picks up her tools and I try to think of something to delay her. Just for a few minutes more. I could drop my sandwich or spill the tea down those nice white bandages. I lift my mug. She turns at the door and waves.

"'Bye, nurse. I hope they send you next time — the end of the week did you say? — I'll be here."

She closes the door, then I remember the sheet.

MUKAI
27 AUGUST

I first heard about the fire on Radio Four six o'clock news. A block of flats in West London had just burst into flames at four this morning. By six in the evening, the pictures in the evening paper showed images of the block — the top half disguised by a blanket of thick black smoke with orange flames shooting upwards. It looked like a painting by an imaginative artist. The article said that the fire brigade had been there for hours, yet nothing had changed. I felt a pang of pity for just a few minutes then an image further down the page of a carnival queen caught my attention. God that woman was fit — in that nice way that working out defines your muscles. I daydreamed about how I'd look on the beach in my bikini. I was looking forward to my workout at the gym, so I was really glad that the traffic was moderate. I made it in time for my spin class. As soon as I walked into the workout area, the air hit me smack in the face ugh! The thick and acrid odours. It's funny that as much as I hated it, that's the thing that really got me into the mood. The vibrant workout gear made me feel happy — red, yellow and cerise, now that's a combination I thought was taking it a touch too far. I watched the sweaty bodies straining against the beat — my tribe, my people. I pushed into the back studio and let the instructor take me through a particularly gruelling session, then I spent a few more minutes on the free weights.

Cancun, here I come!

Whilst I was putting my weights away, I glanced up at the huge screen and was surprised that they were still covering the fire.

Must be even more severe than I'd thought.

When I got home, I found myself developing a morbid fascination with the fire. I sat there flicking through all the news channels, taking it in. My latest David Baldalchi failed to compete with this. I even googled the history of fires in London. Aside from the Great Fire of London, I couldn't find any others that had such a grave impact. The deaths and victims were in the double digits. I was just about to switch to Sky News when I heard a key in the door.

"Hey!" Nate shouted, so I turned the volume down.

"Hey, babe, how was your day at work?" I met him in the kitchen, always his first stop when he got in.

"Great. Yours?" I couldn't hear what he was saying through his mouthful of cold chicken. I watched him drop his rucksack to the floor — the water bottle attached to the side clinked onto the floor.

"That's cold — I'm about to rustle-up something quick. Save your appetite." I got the chopping board out and slid it onto the top of the worktop. I hated that it was my turn to cook, I would rather watch the fire news. I opened and searched the fridge and turned towards Nate, leaving the door open behind me.

I wondered why he was smiling at me.

"Salad or greens?" I asked.

"Salad — I'm heading out again. I'll eat when I get back."

"Oh, where to? I would have started sooner, but I've been sucked in by this fire… "

"Yeah, that's quite serious. I've been following it as well," Nate said, reaching into his rucksack.

"I could swear, you only come home to eat and then rush out again. You aren't… ?" The fridge alarm interrupted me, I closed the door.

"Now, look at what you've done — gone and ruined a perfectly good Insta moment."

"Huh?"

"Just now — when you had the door open, the light was round your afro. It looked like were wearing a halo."

"Huh?"

"Come here, you." He pulled me over and tried to kiss the puzzled look off my face, I responded by standing on tiptoe and meeting his lips with mine. He whispered into my ear "We'll finish this later. I'll be back by nine'ish."

I anticipated later as I watched Nate's caramel-coloured frame lean downwards to pick something out of his backpack as it lay on the floor. While he checked the contents of his wallet, I savoured his profile — his square jaw was bordered by a neatly cut half-beard. Beards were uniform these days. When he first grew his, I hated it but now had come to accept it as one of those things about him that I would never be able to change. At least he never got those cornrows — I hate them on guys. There's no way I'm going to be with a guy that spends more time in the salon than I do. Not gonna happen — definite deal breaker, that one. I hadn't realised that he'd been talking to me.

"Later!" He kissed my cheek and turned to leave.

"Love you, babe!" I don't think he heard me or else he definitely would have answered, love you too, babe. Or would he? He'd been acting offish lately. I didn't want to be the dumpee, I'd rather be the dumper. Maybe I wasn't reading the situation right. I could end up being a little too hasty — didn't want to cut something short earlier than I had to. I mean, there were lots of good bits.

I spied him crossing the road then I speed-dialled Mavis.

"You busy?"

"Not at the moment. What's up?" The silence in the background told me that all her children were tucked in for the night.

"I dunno — I think Nate's seeing someone." I felt myself sounding wooden as I stared at the silent television as if hypnotised by the images that flashed like lightening into the darkened room.

"Paranoia? Or have you got hard evidence?"

"I just get a feeling — you know, intuition and that."

"You need to get yourself a hobby. Or something to occupy your time. Too much thinking about things can be bad for you. You start seeing things that ain't necessarily so!"

"Oh! Stop quoting song lyrics at me — I haven't got time for hobbies and whatnot."

"Make the time!"

"I'll tell you what's taking my attention is that fire. Have you seen it? I've been watching it since I got home."

"What you have is a morbid fascination. Enjoy contemplating the most precise images…

"… of things whose sight is painful to us. Weird though true," I finished.

"Mr Mukona would be proud," she laughed.

"Do you reckon he's still teaching English at Mulberry High School?"

"Who knows? But, seriously though, my cousin — you know the respiratory nurse — says she visits that block all the time. She's got one or two people on oxygen in there. She says she hopes that it wasn't caused by someone smoking near the oxygen cylinder.

"Oh my God! Imagine if someone was smoking near there! It must be awful if you know one of the people that died in the fire. That's my patch, but I only have one or two residents in there."

"It's crazy — I've never seen anything like it. It's still burning, completely out of control."

"I'll talk to you in a bit — they're covering it on Channel Four."

"At last, you've got something to keep your mind busy."

I flicked through the channels and slid my fingers back and forth on my iPad looking for anything new and also to get different perspectives from the public. What did they really think about this fire? By the ten o'clock news, I'd had enough.

My eyes feel square now. To bed. I can't believe he's not home.

I remember hearing Nate arrive at some ridiculous hour. I remember thinking that he was taking liberties. I suppose that's the time I realised how much I love him because I should have stopped him right there — no man of mine is going to be out all hours every night of the week. But he had me, I was weak. I used Terry McMillan's words to get me out of bed.

Too many of us are hung up on what we don't have, can't have, or won't ever have. We spend too much energy being down, when we could use that same energy — at least trying to do, some of the things we really want to do.

I showered, dressed and later that morning, I parked my car near the office and then rushed off to the corner shop before going into work. I could smell the smoke — nothing heavy that would have caused me to cough — just a whiff of it, the wind seemed to be taking it in the opposite direction.

I bet if I go to the shop, there will be people talking about it in there. Maybe I could eavesdrop a little.

"'Morning, Sanjay — did you hear about the fire?" I said, after the bell at the entrance jangled incessantly despite my shutting the door behind me. Sanjay was bending over his deliveries and was trying to cut open one of the deliveries with one blade of a pair of scissors.

"Of course. Hasn't everyone in London?"

Really, Sanjay? Sarcasm?

" I suppose. It's awful. Funny thing is that no one seems to know how it started."

"It was deliberate."

"What do you mean? How can you just say that, Sanjay?"

"My cousin supplies fridges and stoves — that kind of thing — to a shop in the area. He heard something."

"Something like what exactly? Who would want to do such a thing?"

"There are some haters out there. Not everybody. But some people. You have to be careful. I don't know any more than that," Sanjay said, he'd opened the box and was forcing even more papers into a folder that he couldn't close.

"I'm sure it was an accident. Just a terrible accident."

"Not. I tell you something fishy happened there." His eyes kept switching between the door and me. The bell tinkled another new customer in who disappeared into the refrigerated section.

"Not sure I agree with you. I'll take these four papers. Thank you." I added some chocolate bars.

"In time, you'll see." He watched the other customer from the strategically-placed mirror. "Can I help you, mate?" .

"No, you're all right," the man responded, walking towards the counter with his selection of milk and yogurts.

I slipped out into the street and after I'd settled behind my desk, I forgot all about our conversation. By lunchtime, I was totally filled in about how many lives had been drastically transformed or tragically lost.

The fire had raged out of control for twenty-six hours despite the best efforts of the firefighters.

One hundred and fifty people were feared dead — among them the elderly, babies, children, women and men.

Two million litres of water had been sprayed onto the fire.

One thousand canisters of foam were used to deal with the internal flames.

Three hundred and forty people were injured when the fire spread to surrounding houses.

Two hundred and ten families were made homeless.

It was a full-on day by all accounts, but I had this niggly discomfort about Nate. I wondered what he was up to. My thoughts ended up worrying my stomach and constantly reminding me that I had to act. I felt angry, fearful. I really wanted to get away from work — maybe I could do some volunteer work with the fire victims. I suppose it was all too overwhelming for me because I found myself standing outside my manager's office.

"June, how's it going? Got a minute?" I stuck my head round to see if she was in the mood to discuss leave options.

"I've literally got a minute." June looked up at me and then back at the notes beside her keyboard. I took up her invitation and slipped into the chair opposite her. She continued to attack her computer keyboard — if I had sat there for too long, she would definitely have forgotten that I was sitting there. I squinted against the light hoping to read the expression on her face. She reached behind her to ease the blinds down, blocking the sunlight out.

"Better?"

"Thanks. It's warm in here," I squirmed out of my cardigan.

"A minute!"

"Can I take my time owing?"

"I don't know if I can spare you, Mukai." The jabbing of the keyboard stopped just long enough for her to look at me and then back down at her notes.

"But it's time owing. Just a couple of days."

"When?" The keyboard sounded louder.

"I was thinking tomorrow, Friday Monday and Tuesday."

"That's four days." She pounded some more.

"Okay, tomorrow then Friday and Monday."

"Go on then. Make sure you fill out the paperwork so that I can sign you off."

"Ta, June." I rushed to the door before she could add any conditions to the leave.

On the way home, I thought about what else I could do with the time off. It would have been great if I'd been able to go away for a few days. I daydreamed about where to go but couldn't think of anywhere suitable on a minuscule budget. So, I stopped thinking and stared at the people in groups and pairs as they passed, their blank expressions identifying them and tying them to what must have been a horrific night. I wondered where they would sleep, what they had lost and what came next.

I decided that volunteering would be more cathartic than rushing off on a break. It might help me ease off the anxiety about Nate. I didn't want to go home to him, but at least I had somewhere to go, unlike the people from the fire. I trudged up the stairs to the flat and decided to go to bed early to avoid him, without supper, if necessary. I didn't want to fight or even ask him about where he'd been the night before.

"You're home early." Nate zoned in for a kiss. I allowed a light peck on my cheek because I thought it'd be easier than trying to explain why I didn't feel like it.

The sweet garlic-flavoured chicken choked me as I went past the kitchen to leave my lunchbox to soak in the sink.

" Yeah, I didn't go to the gym. What's up?"

"That's not like you."

"I just needed a break."

"I'm making some jambalaya." I made a face when he turned towards the stove.

"Okay, I'm going to have a bath."

I wished I'd locked the door because he followed me a few minutes later.

"Would madam like to have her back washed?"

"I'm okay, Nate. I just want to soak for a bit."

"Are you mad at me about last night?" His fingers felt magical as they worked the knots out in my shoulders and the nape of my neck. This was the trouble with Nate, he just got round things with his magical hands. I soaked into the suds.

"I'm just tired. That's all." I managed a half smile.

" Last night it took a little longer than I expected with James... "

"Huh, till midnight. James must be a great deal more interesting than me." I couldn't let him get away with it.

"It's not like that at all. I'll tell you about it later." He stood up suddenly, "Jambalaya needs my attention." And just like that, he left me hanging.

ABI
12 JANUARY

I'd only been at the bus stop for five minutes, but my toes were frozen. Just two weeks ago, this time, I was already sweating in my wrap and sandals in Lagos. I hoped that soon I wouldn't be here in winter. To make it worse, the bus was late, I shouldn't have run like that.

At last, the number seventy-one arrived, I shook my umbrella and struggled onto the bus, water dripping everywhere. That driver looked at me as if he couldn't see it was raining. When I sat down, I tried not to be too comfortable, ten minutes later, I had to change buses. The next bus was on time. After twenty minutes, I was in Dalston and, for the first time, I arrived at work before seven. Usually, someone was arguing with the driver, but that day everybody was calm. That earlier bus was better, no drama. They started this clock-in business at work to punish those that were late. I wondered if I would get extra money for being early.

Huh?

Who was this? Using my hook and my locker? Must be agency, I didn't know anyone with a furry coat like that. Everyone knew that this was my hook. Of course, I had to move the things. I washed my hands and got my breakfast out of a blue plastic container. I always reuse plastic containers. Ssome of these carers like to buy these fancy, fancy whatsaname — boxes. They like to waste money. I read the writing on the top.

Gelatelli Bourbon Vanilla Ice cream

I didn't remember eating that ice cream. Maybe it was one day when I was extra happy. My breakfast was the same every day — two thick slices of bread, plenty of peanut butter and sweet tea to wash it down, otherwise, that peanut butter can dry the mouth. My phone was ping-pinging in my pocket, so I put it on the table to read the WhatsApp message. It was a video about a Nigerian Pastor in church on Sunday. The church was full, even people standing at the back. All watching. The pastor had his hands up to do a whatisit healing. The ushers were holding the sick man down, and the call came... just as it was getting exciting.

Hey! Who is this now? — Nigeria!

As much as I wanted to, I couldn't ignore the flashing green button.

"Hallo. Ehe?"

He likes to drag things out. How was this? How was that? Trying to butter me. I know him well.

"You found my number?"

"Of course! How can I not have the number for you, my most senior wife?"

"Okorie, am I now your senior wife?" He was definitely trying to butter.

"How can you ask such a thing? Of course. Even though you do me like that. You are still my most prized wife. Mother of my most senior son. The one who will inherit all of this." Okorie was trying to be charming. When I was a young girl, it worked. Heh.

I knew that he was referring to that old house with those thirsty fields around it. I remember working out there in the hot sun while he was out chasing women. He made me want to click, click at him and kiss my teeth — but, I wanted to know what was so important that he should phone me. So, I just made a face at the phone instead.

"So, you phoned me all the way from Nigeria to tell me this?"

"I called you to remind you of your duty. Our mother is not well. In fact, she is very ill."

"Ehe? What is wrong with her?" I felt stabbing in my heart, just here. She is a good woman, wo. I think she felt sorry for me because she also had other wives squeezed into her marriage bed.

"She has very bad pain. The doctors need a scan to see what is wrong."

"Why haven't you sent her for the scan? You are failing in your duty as a son." I heard my voice getting louder. I didn't mean to shout. But it's a small, small thing for him to do.

"Those are very strong words. I know you don't mean them. You are just concerned. But my businesses have not been doing very well. I am not making enough money to do everything."

"Maybe because you have too many wives."

"The line is not good, wo, what?"

"How much is the scan?" I was glad that he didn't hear what I'd said before, I didn't want to start a fight.

"Three thousand Niara. And there are fees for the doctor too."

"You mean you can't find that somewhere?" I was sure that he had a new wife.

"I wouldn't be phoning you if I could."

"Ah! So, I am made of money? I have money-tree in my whaty'call — bedroom?"

"Ah, so harsh. Think of mother."

His voice made my tea sour.

"I'll see what I can do." I pressed the red button; it was enough. Even the video no longer interested me. While I was wondering what to do, the other carers arrived.

I saw Beauty.

"Hello, my sister. I'm sure you're now settled?"

"Yes. How was Nigeria? I thought you weren't coming back."

"I always go for three months. After three months, I will be going back again."

"You must tell me what you are doing. Maybe I can learn something."

"It's nothing really. After I have worked enough shifts, I will buy goods for my shop at home. Then I lock up when I have sold everything and I come back. I am building a place of my own."

"Oh, that's clever!"

I got up and washed my cup whilst I watched Beauty and Yemi fix their lip gloss. I wondered if they thought the residents care about their wigs and make–up. Me, I was always natural.

I liked working with Beauty those days. Especially when we were put on the top floor. They were the heavy residents and we had to do everything for them. But there were only six. So, when we worked quick-quick by the first tea break, we were finished. After our breaks, we sat in the little room to write our progress notes. Beauty talked a lot, about the lazy carers, who had been caught sleeping on night duty. I knew who she was talking about. Me, I never worked at night — I didn't want them laughing at me if I got caught sleeping. Besides I needed to keep the job, wo.

"Abi, I need your help." Beauty had never asked me for anything before.

"Of course. As long as you're not asking for money." I was only joking. I told her about the call from Okorie, we rolled eyes at each other. These men — the cleaner walked in before we could say what we meant.

"Mihaela, how have you been?" I asked her. I moved the papers on the desk to see if she would dust it. Instead, she pulled the plastic bag out of the bin and brought the hoover in. I watched her wipe her nose and then nod, stick her chin out and raise her shoulders, like a chicken — I knew that meant everything is okay.

"Aw. You know, just work. How was holiday, Abi? How was Africa?" Mihaela asked. I had always thought that Romanians had black hair, Mihaela's was a browny-red colour. It was pretty, her skin was very pale. She worked very fast, those long legs and arms. But she was too thin. When she put her hands on her hips, I could see the shape of her hip bones. No African man would tolerate that. But at least she had a husband, and he didn't seem to mind.

"Africa was fine."

"I go also home — next week." Mihaela smiled.

The minute she left, Beauty couldn't wait to ask me,

"And you're going to help him?"

It took me a while to remember what we'd been talking about. Oh yes, Okorie.

"She is a good woman, wo. In fact, I will send the money to his nephew. Then I will be sure that woman will get treatment." I said, hoping that I would be able to see her on my next trip to Nigeria.

"Ah! You're so generous." The buzzer rang. "I'll get it!" Beauty squeezed her big bottom between my chair and the wall. She's getting too big. "You can get the next one." She said, turning from the door. Even her breasts were too big. And that tiny waist — so attractive. Maybe a size twenty. Me, I'm a size sixteen, especially when I've just come back from Africa. Like now. Beauty came back soon after.

"Ah, Mrs Jones! She's asking when her daughter will be in. Have I got a crystal ball?" Heh, Beauty — drama as usual. " But Abi, I really need a flat. I can't stay with those people anymore. They're always late with the rent. They eat my food. And they leave the kitchen dirty. If it was Africa, we would have cockroaches by now. Do you know of anywhere?"

"I can talk to my whatsaname. I know that there is an empty flat on my floor. Let me call him at break." I knew if I referred a new tenant to him, he would give me something.

"How much is the rent?"

"It's six hundred a month. You can easily afford that."

"I thought it was council."

"Yes, it is, but these people get many flats in different names. Then they sublet them. Everywhere is like that. So long as they pay the council — it's okay."

"What if they don't pay?"

"My sister, they will pay — they don't want to lose the flat."

I phoned the landlord before Beauty came back from her break — I negotiated fifty pounds for myself. My bus fare every month.

650? I wrote on a piece of paper.

550, Beauty wrote back.

He agreed to charge her five hundred and seventy-five pounds on the first of each month, with a three-hundred-pounds deposit and she could move in at the end of January. He would get his rent, I would receive my fifty pounds each month and Beauty was grateful for the flat, so everybody was happy.

"Thanks. I'll pay the deposit on Friday. Then I can move in the last weekend of January."

"Don't mention, my sister. Just make sure you're not late with the rent. I don't want my name to be… "

"Of course, Abi. Don't worry."

I think Beauty, she will pay on time.

MUKAI
29 AUGUST

I waited to hear Nate's keys in the front door before opening my eyes. I needed to confront Nate about the late hours he was keeping, but I didn't want to do it first thing and put a negative vibe on the rest of the day. I showered and dressed and was thinking about what I should do next when a text message pinged in.

Damn, forgot to turn off my work phone.

"Need next-of-kin details for BL 26736 thought to have been trapped in the fire.

Can you forward her files, please?"

I remembered Mrs Lyons — Betty. I had interviewed and assessed her about a week ago to arrange carer support for her. The referral should have been actioned by then. I hoped that she hadn't been trapped in her flat when the fire started. Realistically, though, I couldn't imagine that she had been anywhere else.

Even if she had managed to make it to the door, she couldn't move very fast. There's no way she would have made it out of there alive on her own. I remember the guy next door — Paulo — Pab — something, he always looked out for her. Maybe, just maybe, he managed to get her out.

Oh my God — there's no way he would have been able to carry her out.

I grabbed my car keys and rushed out the front door. When I arrived at the west office I ran inside in search of the texter.

"Is Jess around? Jessica, hi. I know I'm meant to be on leave, but I had to come in."

"Ah! You could have just phoned." Jess led the way to a free computer on one of the desks at the far end of the open-plan office.

"I couldn't stop thinking about that poor woman. How awful! So, is she… "

"We don't know yet. Maybe she made it out of there."

"I doubt it, Jess. I just visited her last week and she could barely walk to the front door to open it when I arrived. I made recommendations for a key-safe and package of care. Then I handed her over. I can retrieve the form I completed from here."

We spent a few minutes reviewing her personal information on the form.

"Here it is — next of kin, daughter, Angela. Second contact, Pablo," Jessica read out aloud.

"Oh, that's her neighbour. I remember now, she didn't have any family. Or at least they weren't interested in her. As soon as her daughter got power of attorney, she ghosted — hasn't been back to see her at all. She has a son somewhere, but they haven't spoken in years."

"We'll have to refer her file to the police so that they can try and trace someone. Especially if this guy was also caught up in the fire."

"What can I do to help?" I smiled hopefully, though I suspected Jess was the red-tape type and wouldn't let me help unless she received a signed document from her manager. But it was worth a try.

"Not a lot really." Jess closed the file and removed my smart card from the hard drive.

Well, I supposed that was that.

"Maybe I could try to locate this guy? This Pablo fellow? It's worth a try — besides, I've got time off I could really do some checking around."

"The police are already doing what they can. Other agencies are also involved — you'll only end up getting in the way."

"Well, at least I know what they both look like."

"Oh, why can't things just be straightforward?" Jess said, pushing her glasses further up her nose and smoothing her wiry curls down.

"Just off to the loo." I went in the general direction of the toilets at the back, then left the building via the back door.

I thought the hundreds of images and videos I had seen of the fire and its victims would have prepared me for anything. I was so wrong. It was quite different coming face-to-face with it.

The first thing I noticed when I got out of the car, were the odours of gas, electric wiring, nylon, curtains, plastic and what must be flesh — it was disgusting and got caught in my throat. My imagination painted frightening images of babies suffocating to death, people in flames, burns and the thick black smoke steaming out of the rubble. I circled Babel, respecting the yellow police tape, and stopped just in front of the remains of a ground-floor flat with its crumbly kitchen appliances covered in soot, balancing precariously in the breeze like a shadow waiting to disappear when the light changed. The front door was contorted into bizarre aluminium sculptures.

Who had lived there? The passers-by lugged bags of donated clothing, bed linen and whatever personal belongings they had managed to salvage from the ruins. They didn't appear to have any particular destination in mind as they shuffled forward under the weight of their black bin bags. Reduced to ghosts of themselves — their pasts, present and futures lay in the ashes, being sifted into all directions by the traffic-induced wind.

One woman sat on a bright red leather sofa that she had salvaged from the remains of her home. Its scarlet velvet upholstery was sobered by charcoaled armrests.

I followed the queue of the dispossessed in line for rehousing, food and clothing into one of the buildings that had been converted into temporary refugee administrative hubs. I waited briefly in front of what looked like a reception desk. They were so busy that they didn't even have time to look up from their desks. It was taking them a long time to assist each victim. I gave up waiting.

I decided to try the nearby church hall. The interior was so dark I had to stand in the doorway for a few seconds for my eyes to adjust. The cool air felt soothing after the blistering air outside. I followed the sound of ringing phones and muted conversations.

"Hello, love, resident or next of kin?"

"What?" To my left was a blonde woman of forty-something sitting at a desk a few feet from the entrance.

"Resident or next of kin?"

"Neither. I just thought that I might be able to help."

"Look, love, I don't mean to be funny or nothing. But you have to be specially trained to do what I'm doing."

"I just thought you might need a hand with something."

What training could she possibly have received in just a day? Ridiculous woman.

"I'll tell you what. See that man over there — him with the grey t-shirt? Yes, him, what's scratching his head. Tell him. He might be able to give you something to do."

Before I could reach him, he had moved to the far side of the room, where he talked to a group of young people. I continued towards him, jumping or dodging the piles of clothing or people pouring even more clothes onto the plastic protection on the floor.

"I just wanted to know if I could help. I'm off for a few days, so I could potentially be here every day," I addressed him when he'd finished with the group.

"Marvellous," the man responded, rubbing his hands together. "Come with me. And what are you off from? We can use all the skills we can get." He led the way to yet another room where the noise was even louder.

"Social worker."

"Really? That's brilliant. I have just the job for you." He turned around and me out again. "I'm Jake, by the way."

"Mukai."

"That's an exotic sounding name… " His phone rang over the rest of the sentence.

That first morning, I was glued to a desk logging found identity documents into a spreadsheet. I entered the last passports and then moved onto a pile of papers that miraculously survived the fire. They smelled of smoke and had the crispness of paper that had been wet and dried again. Picking the first one up, I examined it.

Matongo — that sounds like a Zim name. Isn't that Mum's neighbour's surname?

Oh God. I can't make out the first name. Date of birth — they must be about forty-two. Oh my God. I wonder if I could — but it would be a breach of confidentiality — but it's an emergency. Who should I ask? I can't ask Miss-you-can't-do-my-job over there. Jake might know. But I think I need to ask a senior social worker. I'll ring June.

"Quick one, June," I said when a grouchy June answered.

"You want to extend your leave?"

"No, June — I'm holding someone's asylum identity document thingy. I know someone with the same name. Is it ethical or not for me to ask if they knew anyone in that

75

block — you know as a means of identifying them? Or is it breaching?"

"You need to hand the document to the authorities and let them handle it."

"I am the authority, I mean, I'm helping out in one of the offices and my job is to make a record of the documents that have been found. That's why I'm asking."

"That's very good of you, Saint Mukai — is this why you wanted time off?"

" No, I just happened to be passing by and I could see they needed help."

"Well, I don't know the answer to that one."

"Oh, couldn't you… ?"

"No, absolutely not. I've got enough of my own bloody womrk to do. I'll see you when you get back."

I spied a liaison officer from the Met — she seemed approachable.

"I have a dilemma —, sorry let me start again. My name is Mukai. I'm volunteering by keeping a record of all identity documents found in the rubble — I've just found a document — the name on this document — I know someone with the same surname. Would it be appropriate to contact this family to find out if they had any relatives living at this address?"

"Well, love, best thing to do is pass the task on to the local police station. They can pay them a visit and do it that way."

"They don't live around here."

"Oh, right? Where do they live?"

"Zimbabwe."

"Oh! I wouldn't know what they do there."

The chances of the Zimbabwean authorities getting involved were quite remote, so I decided to take matters into my own hands.

"Mama, yes, it's me. Mama, what is the name of your neighbours? Sorry. How are you, mama? Fine. Yes. No, the ones on the left. With the big dog. Matongo. I thought so. Do they have any relatives by the same name living in London? Daughter-in-law? Mum, can you find out? Oh, and get her first name, please. It's important. I'll call you tonight."

The rest of the day seemed to crawl past. When I thought no one was looking, I scanned the document onto my phone.

"What did you decide to do then?" I jumped. That liaison officer had snuck up on me. I made a note to be more careful in future.

"Oh. I just decided to go backwards. I asked for the address of their relative here in London. I thought that way I won't alarm anyone unnecessarily."

"Nicely done. Don't hesitate to contact me if you need my help." She handed over a card. "I'm not always on-site, so you can call me."

I slipped the card inside the cover of my phone alongside all the 'just in case' business cards. There were no more documents to log in so I decided to take a break. I took a slow walk to Fags & Mags as there was no where to sit in the sunshine. People were still walking up and down the pavement, but the traffic was almost at a standstill. The drivers were slowing down to get a good look at the ruins and gain insight into the lives of the affected.

"Hey, Sanjay." I leaned both my elbows on the counter. "I just need to chat,." I said to Sanjay's raised eyebrows.

He went back to the other side of the counter to continue rearranging the bottles in the fridge to make room for more water bottles.

"I've been busy because of all the people in the street. If it's not customers, then it's the police. I've been robbed by those yobs a few times already today."

"Oh, Sanjay, I'm sorry to hear that. It wasn't — I mean, you didn't get hurt?"

"No, nothing like that. Just kids taking advantage of the chaos." He shrugged and continued to reshuffle bottles. I wondered if he was doing that just to keep busy.

"Not working today?"

"No, but I've been helping out at the support centre they set up. It's so depressing."

"All caused by some very bad people."

"You keep saying that, Sanjay."

"Well, I told you… "

The entrance alarm chimed and Sanjay fell silent. His attention focused on his security mirrors and cameras where his eyes followed the newcomer around the crowded shop. Two more shoppers arrived shortly afterwards. I paid for a carton of coconut water and headed back to the centre. They were serving food parcels for lunch. I found a spot to stand and help. I got chatting to a man who had lost his wife and young child. His wife usually worked the night shift, but they had changed around so that she could attend an evening course. He was at work when the fire broke out.

"It should have been me." His voice broke and his eyes seemed to swell — a small drop raced down onto his brown paper bag with his sandwich, packet of crisps and a banana. The parcel silently slid to the floor, I imagined it splintering into tiny shards, each one slicing a heart in two.

BEAUTY
28 JANUARY

I felt sad to be leaving, but it was too much, I wasn't used to sharing and what-what. I was going to miss them — especially Fungayi, who was always making funnies and Shorai, busy with the latest news from home — she should have got a job with ZIANA.

They made me feel bad about moving out, but I promised to call them. I was looking forward to moving. It's true, I hadn't seen the new flat — I didn't expect much. I had a feeling inside that it would be better.

I booked a cab for nine o'clock. The mini-cab driver was a bit late, well, he came at half-past, but I was still moving the five boxes and three suitcases to the front door when he arrived, so it was okay. Funny, normally, one or two people were at home at this time on a Saturday. Nobody was there to help. And the driver took his time to get out of the car. He just opened the boot and then picked up one or two boxes,

Some people!

I made myself comfortable in the back seat between the small boxes that couldn't fit the boot. I watched the meter — it was talking in pounds. They'd said thirty pounds. If it was more, he'd see me! I would perform.

"What place is this?" I kept asking the driver, every time I saw another small Tescott. I think the third time I asked him he got cross.

"I'll tell you when we get near." His voice sounded rough. I needed his help when we got there, so I decided to keep quiet.

At last, I saw a tube station, White City, and I knew that was in West London. I hoped we were nearly there. While we were stopped at the traffic lights, I watched people going into the underground. It was early, but they already looked tired. I was glad I wasn't going to work that day. The snow just makes you feel tired especially with all those clothes you have to wear, they just weigh you down.

When we moved on, I tried to pay attention so that I could see when we'd arrived. I couldn't see the names of all the flats so when the driver slowed the cab down in front of this old, dirty building, I wanted to cry. Then we started moving again, and I sniffed the snot back. There was a block that looked nice; maybe this new place was a poshy place. I could see myself coming out of those flats with all the glass around the bottom. I hoped it was that one, but it was number one hundred and seventy-nine, so we passed it. At last, I saw the building, "BABEL" a big sign on the front with a small lawn.

"Here, here!" The driver kept going, I'm sure he was trying to get another pound. "I said, here!"

He stopped and turned in his seat.

"I was looking for somewhere safe to stop. I can't park here for long. There should be somewhere to turn in. There's usually parking at the back."

After he had made a few more pounds, we found it — a small road to the back on the street behind. It wasn't as nice as the glass one. But it was better than that dirty, old one that had almost made me cry. The snow was melting, so everything looked like white paint coming off. Once all the snow had melted, I'd get to see everything.

I remember looking up. I had seen them before, those high-rise things but I never thought I'd live in such a tall building — we didn't have these in Zim. I would have to learn to live in the sky, like a bird. The spaces between the windows were painted green, purple and pink — maybe they were meant to look like flowers. There was lots of space outside, but it was hard, cement everywhere. Even the parking spaces were cement   big boxes pressed against the walls. It didn't look friendly, maybe that's why there was bright paint everywhere. I hoped it would look better in summer. I wondered what it would be like inside. First, I had to worry about getting my things inside.

"What did you say your name is? Asa?" I asked the driver.

"Asad."

I admired his curly hair and browny-black complexion. Maybe he was from Somalia or Ethiopia. He was handsome, like a girl. I wondered if he was enough of an African brother to help an African sister.

"I'm Beauty — from Zim."

"Ah, my sister — Zimbabwe. I'm from Eritrea." Well, at least he's my brother.

We turned to the concrete frames to decide where to park. Asad chose the one near to the back door and reversed into it. The locks on the doors clicked open as he took the key out. I waited, for the door to slide open, like magic. He jumped out and put my suitcases and boxes beside the door. I paid him.

"If you could help me put them in the lift?" I tried to open the door. Asad took the keys and pressed the plastic thing on the side, and the door opened — ah ah! I smiled at him.

"Okay, but quick, huh!" He kept the door open with one of the boxes, "Which floor?"

"Let me… seven, seventh floor."

The floor was cement up to the lift. The front reception looked pretty with the big, black tiles that shone so bright — that part reminded me of home. Just a bit. We had a kitchen with a cement floor, and we put black polish and shined and shined until I could see my face. I stopped feeling so nervous.

Asad was in charge of getting us upstairs. He pressed up for the lift. We hadn't waited long when lift number four arrived. I ran towards it, pulling a suitcase. The door opened and I checked inside the lift. It had a black rubber floor with squares that you could catch small wheels between. We managed to get the three suitcases and five boxes inside. When the doors closed, the smell was powerful — maybe Dettol or something like that. Asad made a face then sneezed.

"Hmm, at least it's clean." I was trying to make him stay with me.

"Too much," he said. I wondered what kind of house he lived in. And what his wife bought for cleaning. Me, I like Dettol. Kills germs. I passed him a tissue. I hate it when people just wipe on their shirts. *Sies*.

On the fourth floor, the lift started shaking.

Oh, my God!

I grabbed Asad's shoulder. I think he didn't like that. I mean he is quite skinny and my hand — well, it's quite big. He started pressing buttons, even the one with a phone on, the one for emergency. Then the doors opened. I ran out and helped Asad pull everything from the lift. I made sure I was standing outside the lift just in case the doors got stuck.

We made so much noise, I think we must have disturbed people in their flats. I was concentrating on pulling and pushing, then I stood up and turned around. I mean, I didn't mean to scream. It wasn't nice, but she gave me such a fright, standing there like a ghost, her white hair flying around her head like that. When she walked, she looked like she was being pushed, like flying. When I remembered my manners, I walked towards her.

"Good morning, Mama."

"You movin' in? You sure you got the right floor — this one's full up y'know."

"The lift won't go up." Asad pointed at the lift, the door lying open like a hungry bird.

"That's the only one that's working." I think she was Jamaican. "I haven't been out for a week now. My legs won't let me do the stairs. It's not safe for me y'know."

"Wait here," I told Asad. I moved one of the suitcases to the stairs.

I had to stop every ten steps to change the suitcase to the other arm. I counted seven steps before I could rest and look out the window. The windows were dirty where the snow had left some stains. Inside the sill, there were cigarette butts and matches. I looked at the signs on the doors that lead onto each floor. It was there — No Smoking!

So, it was clear that some of the people there didn't listen. Maybe the young ones. No discipline.

I tried to open the window even though it was cold outside. It's hard when you're panting like a dog and the air is thick with Dettol and other strong smells. I couldn't get my breath back. But at least it showed that someone did come to clean, or try to clean. For those who don't care about these things, it was okay.

I stopped to rest for the last time before I went through the door on the seventh floor and something made me look down the stairs. Near the fourth floor there was a young black boy that came out of the door onto the stairs. He packed something inside his sweatshirt, then zipped his coat. He looked up. I know he saw me. Maybe he was hoping I didn't know what was in the parcel he was hiding.

He turned away and ran down the steps. Before he got to the bottom, the same door opened and two older black boys ran out. There was shouting and banging of doors. I hoped that it wasn't always going to be like that.

"Ahh!" I said to myself. Then I opened the door to my new life.

I looked around. It looked clean, nothing special but Abi had told me that at least someone came to sweep and mop. The strong smell of cleaning was better here. I walked down to flat number seventy-seven. There were doors on both sides, three on the right before I got to mine. I wondered who else lived here. I knew Abi's was the first on the right, number seventy-one.

The front door was clean, at least. It was easy to unlock it. Before I opened it, I had to breathe. I only wanted a small one-bedroom. As long as it was only for me, no sharing, I could take anything.

There was a small space just inside where I could hang my coat. Three doors in front of me. I wondered which one to open first. I decided to start on the left.

Oh! This one was big. I didn't think I'd have such a big lounge. I could get a small dining table to put at the end. I could eat there and look out of the window, it would be fun to see people walking far, down there. On the left, there was a small kitchen, with shelves around the top and bottom. A stove was right in the middle. I turned it on to check if it was working.

Yeess!

A bit dirty, but I would clean it. I just had to buy a fridge and a microwave. I went back to the lounge. I thought I'd get a white leather suite — I would put the sofa across that wall on the right and the chairs facing in a square. A small coffee table in the middle. Yes, there was space to pass through to the kitchen. But the carpet needed to be changed. No children, so even a cream one was okay.

I touched the walls and the shelves and wondered if I had enough Dettol and Flash.

The other room was a bedroom — a big one to fit a double or even a king-size bed. It was better than my old bedroom, where I had a single bed. It's hard for a big girl like me to turn, just like that. I need space to turn. There was something smelling — it was a stained, dirty mattress. I had to close my nose. I opened the window and looked out.

Across the street was a big house. Like the ones in the low density in Harare. I couldn't see the front door properly, because there was a big tree in front of it. The branches were spread wide. I thought about the mazhanje tree at my house in Chinoyi, Zim.

Yah man! There was definitely someone there. I wondered what kind of person lived there. It must be very nice inside. I was standing there, just imagining, when I heard a lorry down there. The driver was busy toot, tooting at someone in front. That's when I remembered Asad.

I just managed to check the bathroom quickly. A bath and a shower. Good! But the light was finished, so I couldn't see it properly.

Asad helped me with the rest of the things.

"Thank you, Brother Asad. Next time I call you first."
I gave him ten and when he gave me a big smile, I thought
about his wife and children and gave him another five.

"Ah, my beautiful sister, thank you. Here's my
number." And he put his card on the counter in the kitchen.

When he had left, I thought I needed music, as always,
to clean thoroughly. I found the wireless speaker and blue-
toothed a Zimbabwean music playlist that Shorai had sent
me from Spotify.

Ah, yah!

I worked hard for three hours, just to make it clean.
Then I opened the windows and sprayed air-freshener. I
only had kitchen things and my clothes, so I unpacked
them. That night I would sleep on the floor, at least it was
warm in there.

I decided to leave the dirty mattress at the back
outside. I hoped the dustman would collect it later. I didn't
want to get stuck in the lift with that smelly thing so I
dragged it towards the green fire door, written 'exit' where
I had just come. I knocked someone's door with it.

Very sorry.

But I was sure that no one was there. I was just about
to open the door to the stairs when the door to flat seventy-
five opened, and a medium woman with grey hair came
out. I wondered if this was a place for mainly old people.

This woman had pink cheeks, they made her look
kind. So, I smiled at her. Before I could say that I was
sorry, she opened her mouth.

"What do you want?"

If I had met her a few months ago, I would not have understood her. I also wasn't used to rude people.

"Nothing."

"So, what d'you bleeding well knock for?"

"I didn't — maybe it was this." I showed her the mattress.

"I suppose you're moving in?" She tried to walk to me, but the bandages on her legs almost tripped her. So, she just stood there. I am sure her blood pressure went up.

"More bloody foreigners. This time coloured ones."

"Whaa…?"

Then she slammed the door. She had called me coloured. I am African, not coloured. Even she, with her old eyes, could see that?

I pushed the mattress through the door so hard I tore it on the door handle — the stuffing came out of it with some black things in it, I thought I saw them moving. I had to be quick and get rid of it. I pulled the mattress down the first few floors, then I met the three black boys from before. They were standing in front of the door to the third floor. This time they were arguing about their deals. 'You owe me — what, what.' They stopped when they saw me standing on the stairs above them.

"'Scuse me!" I waited a second. They had their underpants peeping at me because their jeans were too low. They had matching clothes. Red t-shirts and navy-blue hoodies with the same trainers in black. Maybe the tall one was nineteen, the other two — maybe eighteen.

"Excuse me, please!" This time louder. I was getting angry again.

"Use the lift." The tallest guy said, "Africans!" His bottom lip curled down onto his chin. "You know what a lift is?" They all laughed. I wondered where their mummies were.

"It's not working."

"You want to make somethin' of it yeah?" The shortest one ran up the stairs to me, trying to act tough. He reminded me of my brother's son. I had to sort him out — he was getting too big for his shorts. My brother had been away, and his wife texted me — Simba did what-what, rude what-what. Me, I took a kombie there by five. All I know is she has no more problems with him.

"Look, I'm tired — just let me past." I didn't want things to get worse. But if I ran away now. it was going to be a problem for me.

The tallest one answered his phone, and he opened the door behind him. When he went that side by the lifts, the two other boys tried to show me that they had power.

"Oh, poor you. You hear her, Duwayne, she's speaking in her best English. It's not going to help you, bitch."

"Yeah, fuck off!" Duwayne's eyes looked funny. Maybe he'd been smoking some ganja.

"Make me fuck off." I knew that I could handle Shorty. I was times three of him. Then there was Duwayne — just a bit of boxing would sort him out. Too late, I noticed something shiny in his hand.

Duwayne came towards me, I kept my eye on the knife and thought about what I should do. I could hear the other guy was still on the phone. Far from where we were. I had to be quick. Those two were below me on the staircase — Duwayne on the left, Shorty right.

I had started it, now I had to finish it. If I was angry enough, I could do it. I remembered the coloured thing that woman said. I made myself think about the father of my children to get the heat to my head and I was just feeling it getting a little hot. How he started to bring other women to our home even when he knew I was there. He wanted to show me that he had power and that me — I was nothing. Then the one called Duwayne turned and smiled down at Shorty.

"Checkmate!" He was showing us all his teeth, especially the gold one.

I was ready.

I threw the mattress onto Duwayne and his knife.

"Argh! *Bratishiti! Ndinokumamisa*! Bloody shit! I'll beat the shit out of you!" I screamed, my head was over, over-heating. I remembered the time when my ex brought another woman into the home. He said she was his aunt. I spent two months cooking for her and making her comfortable before I discovered she was his girlfriend. My head exploded into my arms.

The mattress was thick, I didn't feel anything.

I heard him hit the wall.

Dabh!

Like that. His head and his clothes rubbed against the wall as he ended up on the floor. Sitting. Just sitting behind the mattress, like that. All that big man talking — all finished. I quickly turned and sent a punch to Shorty. I missed.

"Hah!" Shorty laughed.

I caught him with my left arm and pushed him hard. He fell down the stairs, and I also fell — I was on top of him. That wasn't good for him.

"Fuck!" Shorty said.

We didn't go to the bottom, as soon as we stopped, I grabbed his collar and pushed him against the wall. I didn't give him a chance to stand straight. I just started bashing him around the head with my right fist.

"Yah! Stay there. I'll sort you."

He put his hands over his head, just like that. I'm sure he was thinking of his mummy. Yah! Let him think. I was doing her job.

"Aagh!"

I pulled him down the stairs some more and then I body-slammed him into the wall, just like WWF.

"Okay, I'm so... "

"Next time... shit!" I was out of breath then. He went down. You know, like on television. By that time, my hands were bleeding. They started paining.

I was scared that other one would come back. Ah! By that time, I was finished. I went back for the mattress. When I lifted it, I was surprised that the knife was so big in his hand. He was just lying there in the corner, and there was blood there on his head. Not a lot. But it could have been bad. I kicked him — just a little. He didn't move, so I checked his pulse by pressing inside his wrist, like Nurse Katie at work did sometimes when we weren't sure if a resident had checked out. I felt something dom, dom like that, hitting my fingers without stopping. So, he was okay.

Better!

I dragged the mattress down past Shorty. He moved, so I waited to see what would happen. Nothing. So, I left.

"*Kurumidza*! Hurry!" I kept saying to myself. I could hardly walk.

I decided to take the lift from the next floor because when Asad and I came it worked up to the fourth floor. I kept watching the door to the stairs. When the lift pinged and the doors opened, I didn't care who was inside, we were going together. As long as it wasn't that long boy who was on the phone.

Another teenager in the lift — it was a she. She was trying to be clever — staring at me because of the mattress. She blink-blinked those fake eyelashes at me. I stared back. Then she flicked her long black weave behind her back and chewed as if she thought she could take me on. If only she knew.

She must have heard me thinking — she suddenly looked at my hands. Then looked down at her phone. She started texting. Quick messages. Quick answers. When the lift opened, she waited quietly for me to leave.

I left the mattress at the back, there where Asad had parked his car. Maybe the snow and rain would make it clean. Who knows?

Me, I was scared to go back to the flat. At my job, we had police checks every year. If the police were there, they would definitely know it was me, then it would be there in my police check next time. I went outside the front. At least I had put on my coat when I went out. I could find anywhere to hide. But I wanted to see what would happen.

I remembered the tree that I had seen across the road, in front of the big house. There was a small wall in front of the house, so I sat there. It was cold, but it would be dark soon, I'd just have to wait. The ground was wet and, ah yah, I thought about being back in Zim.

"Hey! What are you doing there?"

I stood up and, lucky I was tired by then, so it wasn't very fast, or I would have knocked him out. His black overcoat was too heavy for him, it looked like it was sucking all the energy out of his body. He had small hair on the sides of his head.

"Sorry, I thought you were… "

He kept coming step, stop. Like that.

"Why are you sitting on my wall? Are you lost? New carer?" He fixed his jacket and made his shirt collar straight, trying to look like the boss.

"I'm just sitting here. Tired." I hoped he would leave me alone.

The old man kept coming. I knew this would end badly. I didn't want anyone coming to help him, then see me. Next thing, he tripped over a crack, trying to get close. I suppose he couldn't hear me.

I jumped up. Yah! I was tired, but what could I do? I grabbed his arm under mine, like this. Then I took him back up to his door. He looked up at me. The black and grey hair in his nose moved, he was breathing hard.

"Thank you. You're a very strong girl."

Smelly cigarette mouth.

We stood there like that. He was waiting. I was waiting. Then I decided.

I pushed the door and took him in. The passage was dark, I could see a light at the other end, just after the stairs. He pointed towards it, so I took him there.

We were in the kitchen. I made him sit down on the chair by the table. He had left the oven door open and it breathed hot air. I saw an old map on the wall.

"Northern Ireland." I read across the top. 'Beal Feirsde' at the bottom.

"Is that your home?"

He nodded.

"Catholic?" I asked when I saw the cross on the wall.

"Is that a problem?"

"No. I can just ask, can't I?"

He was busy making nice a dishcloth, on the table trying to fold it. It had a picture of a hand that must have been red when it was new. It had become pink from washing. I wondered if his wife had bought it a long time ago. I stopped by the shelf on the window to take a closer look at the black and white photographs with silver frames.

The big one showed four people squashed into a brown sofa. Their hair combed down with gel, all looking like it was bad to smile.

"Oh, that's you!" I pointed at the tallest boy on the side. "Mum and dad? And your brother? Ah, that must be a very, very old picture."

He didn't answer, so I decided I should maybe leave or offer to help him with something. He told me his name was Liam McAuley. He lived alone and hadn't eaten a hot meal for two days.

"How come?"

"Nora hasn't set foot in here for two days. She's been with me for the past fifty years. She always cooks my meals."

"Did you phone her?"

"Today, someone from the hospital called to say that she won't be coming back. She fell and broke her hip. I'll have to go and visit her — Charing Cross. If you can cook and clean — the job's yours."

I supposed I could do it, maybe part-time with Abi. I knew how much she liked money.

"You'll have to bring references."

"No problem. How much are you paying?"

He said ten, I said thirty. He said, split the difference. I now know what that means. Twenty for an hour three times a week. Maybe two more to do the cleaning. Nora had done a good job. My knuckles throbbed. The kitchen tap drip dripped and I tried to close it.

"You been in a fight?" Liam asked.

"So, what do you want for supper?" I asked, rolling up my sleeves. I washed my hands in cold water. It helped the pain, but the soap made it sting.

"I haven't got cash today — so come back tomorrow."

"Just relax, okay? Today is for free. You might as well taste my cooking. What if you don't like it?"

I found two sausages getting thirsty in the fridge and a packet of frozen peas in the freezer. Liam disappeared for a loo break. By the time he got back, the sausages were spitting in the oven. He watched me peel two large potatoes and cut them into small pieces. When I added olive oil and salt, he had a problem.

"You don't need to add oil to potatoes — whatever next."

"There's only one chef — let me do my job."

"It's wasteful."

"Where's the gravy powder?" He didn't know so I dropped a large tomato from the fridge into the water with the potatoes. The skin started to separate from the flesh, the steam was burning my cuts while I was trying to get them out of the pot. I know it smelled tasty because he was quiet while I finished cooking.

I lowered the heat and wiped down the table and laid a place for Liam. I liked to watch the butter melting in the potatoes and the potatoes sucking up all the milk. It was like the end of a really happy story. I stood watching him eat. First a little mash on his fork, then sausage, mash and peas together. Sweet, crunchy, dry, soft juicy and salty all together.

"And?"

"I don't need to be supervised — I'm not one of those unpredictable old fogies. Still have all my faculties."

"What do you think?"

He started using the fork like a hoe to dig up mash for his mouth. I took two of his paracetamols from a plastic container with all his pills. I showed him.

"Look, you've paid me for today. See you tomorrow."

Outside, I could see the blue lights on the ambulance going round and round. It was parked in front of Babel. I hoped that none of the boys would see me. I checked my phone, it was five-thirty. An hour just like that, with the old man. Then I noticed the police car just before it left. I saw one of them in the back of the ambulance. I could tell by his red t-shirt. He had a white bandage around his head. The machine on his arm peeped into the dark. The medic bent over him then they put him into the back of the ambulance. Waiting in the cold was better than meeting them somewhere. I sat on the wall behind the tree again. Nothing much happened. A few people went in and out.

Then I saw Shorty. He was talking on his phone and looking about.

I wondered whether he was looking for me.

ABI
13 JUNE

The flight back from Lagos was packed and noisy. I was glad when we landed at Heathrow. At least the weather in London was better than when I'd left. My flat was just the same when I got there. I showered and slipped on my favourite *Bubu*. It is blue cotton with flowy kaftan sleeves. It made me comfortable whilst I unpacked my small suitcase.

I always kept the flat simple. All the nice furniture was in Nigeria. I just had a brown carpet on the floor in the bedroom and lounge. I had managed to squeeze a black sofa on the side. I never had a lot of visitors, so I found it unnecessary to put any other chairs there. But I bought a coffee table with black glass and gold, just in case someone came. Just to make it look a bit nice, I thought a few pictures would be okay. I got them from Ikea — two of them of red flowers. The two with pink flowers were in the bedroom. I only spent a tenner on everything. I like gold, so they both had gold frames. My friend bought me a gold and brown bowl to put on my coffee table with some fruit. I saw at work, they have those fake flowers in a vase, so I copied — they were also from Ikea. I matched with brown and red curtains in the living room. I don't have a TV because I don't watch that EastEnders or Coronation Street — they are always fighting — but sometimes I watch Nollywood on my tablet.

I started dusting in the bedroom. I prefer whatsyname blue in the bedroom because it's cool. So, I had white sheets and a duvet with blue flowers. I bought the curtains at that linen shop on the high street, deep blue. There was not much space in there for anything much as I used to keep my boxes in there — the things I sold at home, they were full in there. Just simple things here, wo.

I let the water run from the shower to kill all the spiders. Then I put my light blue towels on the rail. Whenever I got back from Lagos, it was hard to cope because it was so quiet. There I had relatives and school friends coming, coming all the time. Especially my brother's three children. They kept me cooking and supervising. I wished I could put all that laughter and sunshine in a bottle to enjoy when I got back to London. It was a hard life, wo.

It was best to keep working, so I phoned the agency.

"Hi it's Abi — Abiola — yes. I just got back today. I'm ready to go back. Yes."

I waited for the consultant to check my file.

"Yes, I can go for my training — anytime. Just book me and tell me yeah?"

I went out to the shops and while I was walking, I started calculations for the things I needed to buy —— seventy dresses;   fifty pairs of shoes and matching handbags; two hundred necklace and whatsyname sets and seventy shapewear pants — last time I got them for seven pounds each. I found I needed at least ten thousand pounds by November so that I could fly back for Christmas. It was the shop's busiest time. My head was full of the number of hours I needed each week. I almost walked past Beauty without seeing her.

"Abi, have I changed so much that you didn't recognise me?" Beauty looked upset.

"I'm sorry, Beauty. I was thinking, wo — so much to do back home."

"How was Nigeria? I was coming to see you because I remembered you'd be back today. You told me, remember?"

"Nigeria is always good, my sister. One day you must come with me."

"And the family? How are they? And your shop?"

"Doing well. Praise God."

"So, who is running it while you are here?"

"I can't leave anyone to run it." I click-clicked. This Beauty, she didn't know about these things. "I sell everything then I lock up. Now, I am thinking about what I would like to sell for Christmas. I need the money — you know I am building two houses — that takes money. A lot of money." I click-clicked as I thought about all that work.

"When are you coming back to work?"

"Maybe at the end of next week. I'll see you later, I'm just going out to buy food. My fridge is empty."

"You must be tired. I've cooked rice and chicken, come. Let me know when you're back."

I went to Beauty's, then went home for an early night. As I lay in the dark, I felt irritated about all the time that I would be wasting away from work; I had to wait a few days for the training and then, only then, I would be able to start work.

I should go and pray about it. Maybe at church, pastor can give me seed blessings so that all of this could work out well.

On Saturday, I went for my whatsaname training. Then in the afternoon, I went to Beauty's flat, to hear all the work news. Just when I was getting comfortable, Beauty said she had to visit someone at Charing Cross — I didn't believe her. I wondered what secrets she was hiding.

As I went back to my flat, I was shocked to hear Betty's television was so loud, even with her door closed door. I could just stand there and listen to the whole show.

I went to sit by the window in my flat to look at my numbers on my tablet and google suppliers. It was still light outside so when I finished, I just watched the cars passing outside and read my WhatsApp messages until it was time for bed at nine.

The next morning was Sunday and I woke up thinking about the prayers the pastor could do for me. It took one-and-a-half hours to get to church, but it was worth it. I had followed the pastor when he moved to this new place. First one bus into the city then east to Leyton. As usual, I was one of the first to arrive, so I waited with two other women until the doors opened.

The church building used to be a warehouse so it was big enough. Every Sunday, at least five hundred people came for our Pentecostal service. Mostly our people from Nigeria and a few Ghanaians. This time of year I liked to see all the women in their traditional outfits. The bright patterns reminded me of pretty flowers thrown together like that. When the women weren't looking, I took photos of the ones I really liked. One of them, I think they call a skater dress. It was deep, deep purple with yellow, light blue and pink patterns. The material was African wax fabric — it really stood out like that. Then I saw a pale yellow and navy blue dress — it just went straight down. It had big patterns. That was nice. One of the ushers had this maxi dress with small, small leaves everywhere on top of these thick lines of blue, red and green material round it just at the bottom — across like this, this. I also liked what I was wearing. An A-line midi-dress with lantern sleeves. Very popular these days, lantern sleeves. I bought the material — a tiger orange with electric blue diamonds around the waist and hem, at whatsyaname, Liverpool Street. I patted my matching headscarf. At last, the man with the keys came — he was late as usual. I didn't bother saying anything. What does it change wo?

I had an important job as an usher in the church. Pastor Kemi liked me to concentrate on the collection bowls. I used to make sure everyone had a chance to tithe. It was true what he said.

"Tell them it's the only way they can gain favour with God."

So, I made sure that I shake-shaked the bowl to get their attention.

I had a few friends at church, but I only saw them at church events. Except for one, Brother Kujoe or just Kujoe, as he liked me to call him. We once had lunch at Nando's but it was just lunch. He was a bit slow — this Ghana man.

As I was going round, I saw him on the far side of the church, preparing to bring the people in. I went straight there.

That's funny — I didn't notice that before.

"Hello Brother Kujoe, it's nice to see you."

"Really, Abi, you must call me Kujoe. Brother is too... too, well, you know what I mean, eh?"

"Congratulations on your marriage."

"Wha... what marriage?"

"I should ask you — that ring on your finger — wedding ring?"

"Oh that, you misunderstand — it's just — a ring. She's in Ghana — we don't really see each other much."

"I see. Well, I am also married — my husband and I — well, it's complicated."

"It gets lonely here — just to have someone to eat with would be nice. If you're free after, maybe we can find something to eat. Like we did last time — you remember, eh?"

The drummer in the choir tapped his cymbals to start the first song.

"I'll see you later." I found my place at the back where I could think.

The whole service, I couldn't stop looking at Brother Kujoe's bald head. He was far there in front. But I kept looking at his head. I don't know why, it wasn't special.

I thought perhaps I can see how it works out. Men from Ghana can be very nice wo!

I stood outside chatting with the others after the service. I admired more dress designs in Ankara, waxed fabrics and lace, as the women walked away from the church. I tried to save some more ideas for the tailor. At last, Kujoe came out. The light blue dhashiki he was wearing and the bright sunlight made his blue-black skin really shine. I remembered the ebony sculptures I bought from Malawi and sold in the shop one time.

"Now, we eat." His teeth looked ready to begin eating something.

He took me to his polished car nearby, one of those new Toyota cars, it was very clean inside.

"Today, we eat Ghana style."

"I've tasted Ghanaian food — it's nice." At least I wasn't going to pay for this food.

When we arrived at Golden Beaches, the Ghanaian restaurant, I looked up and thought I saw a face I recognised at the window. The inside looked like an African place — maybe somewhere on the Gold Coast — thick wooden floors, pretty and shiny. There was space for dancing in the middle. On the left side were small tables for eating. The door at the back was for the barbecue place and Kujoe wanted us to get meat and fish barbecued. So we went outside where Kujoe talked to the man in his language.

Then we went upstairs to wait for it. I couldn't believe it — there was Beauty.

"Hello, Abi!" Beauty was waving. Her table was full, so we couldn't fit. But I didn't really want to sit with her.

"Fancy meeting you here."

"I know, Abi, I was invited by some friends. Just for a quick something to eat." Beauty wanted to dance to the next song but the speakers were too loud. Was this place a nightclub?

"I love this song!" Beauty started moving — quite good for a big person. One of the men from her table got up.

"Come, my Beauty, let's dance." He pulled her towards him, I watched them. I'm sure they knew each other well — like in the Bible.

I turned to Kujoe, he didn't seem like the type who liked dancing. I was glad because I don't go to nightclubs. It's for those young people.

"There's a table over there." He pointed to the back of the room. I continued to stare at Beauty. I suppose she was a good dancer.

"You know that woman?"

"We work together and she lives at my place — she's drunk I think. Maybe that's why she's showing off."

Kujoe didn't seem to have heard, he didn't respond, instead, he talked about what he had on his mind.

"I would like to see more of you, you know."

"But I am still married, and you said yourself, that you are married."

"That makes it even better — because we will both be at ease. I won't pressure you and you also… "

"I see, but you know that's not easy for women. You men can do it. In fact, you do it all the time."

"But, you said yourself — your husband is not here. Let's just enjoy!"

"I need to think about it." I concentrated on removing the meat from the fish bones. It was soft, soft and the hot pepper; it was just enough.

"What about a drink?"

"You mean alcohol?"

Kujoe laughed and then took my hand.

"Relax — anything you want. Perhaps since you're not a drinking person — like me, a little cider would be okay?"

"Malt — get me some malt." I removed my hand, he suddenly seemed to be rushing. I turned to watch the dancers.

That Beauty, she really thinks she's it.

All the men at Beauty's table were competing for her, she just smiled at them. Kujoe could be useful. I hadn't had a man for a while. I invited him in when we got to my flat. I told him that it didn't mean anything — I didn't want to be alone.

This better be worth it!

BEAUTY
16 JUNE

I remember that day it was hot, even at home it doesn't get like this. When I was coming back from the shops, I saw my face in the shop window — it was shining from sweat and the next thing the foundation would be dripping. That's the time you bump into someone that you really wanted to impress. I had no tissue. Lucky it was cool when I got inside Babel. It wasn't easy living at Babel — at any time, those boys I gave a hiding could just find me and that could end badly for me. My friend said I shouldn't have hit them because maybe they're part of a gang where they can even kill you. Next time, maybe the WWF stuff won't work.

Upstairs, the corridor on my floor was empty and quiet except for number seventy-five's television.

Are you a homeowner?

I hated that advert and the ones that were always asking for donations for Africans — all I know is, we don't leave our children dirty like those in the adverts. Anyway, when I shut my front door, I couldn't hear it anymore. I opened the kitchen window and I stood there to let the cool air go down my dress and I drank a big glass of water, just like that, without stopping.

I checked my shopping; six hundred grams bony beef — heh, that's what the butcher called it — green leafy vegetables that reminded me of tsunga from home, two medium-sized onions, a can of chopped tomatoes, beef stock because, of course, there's no royco-usavi-mix around here.

The beef sizzled in my special garlic, ginger powder and Raji curry powder marinade. I let it turn brown, you know, like toast. The chopped onion reminded me of jewels around the meat. I once had a necklace like that. Then I put tomatoes that looked like the cushions in my living room. They swam round and round together like that in juices. I hated cutting the greens, because it took so long, but I liked them thin, like cotton, so I had to do it. I got out my other pot especially for greens and I cut the onion, same like the greens. I watched the tomato and red sweet pepper cubes dancing in the hot frying pan, they reminded me of the way that we danced at Aunt Rhoda's wedding at Chinoyi Technical College. I covered them with the shredded greens — thin emerald-green threads, that you could knit into a jumper and sew on ruby buttons.

Jah Signal was on Spotify, the cubed speaker on the windowsill was really bringing him.

Ah Sweetie, shinga murora
waka wuya wega ko gara pano
Ah Sweetie, shinga murora

All that was missing was the noise of my children playing outside. I put the meat in a casserole dish to finish cooking in a hundred and eighty degrees of oven heat. My phone rang, then stopped.

Harare — what now?

I got my phone card and dialled the number, hoping it wasn't anything serious.

"Ko — I was going to phone you later. Ko chi? Is everything all right?"

"Sis, we're fine. How are you? It's just Maita — she says you promised to teach her how to cook sadza." It was my sister who looks after my kids.

"That wasn't the plan — but it's okay. Let me call."

I made a WhatsApp video call — the phone standing against the container of mealie meal.

"Eh!"

"Hoza Friday!" My sister, Viada shouted. "Here's Maita."

"Hello Mama — you promised to teach me how to cook sadza." Maita had her father's complexion and his nose. Medium brown, round face and quite big. Well, it could be from me also. I'm big. Her hair was up in two bunnies. I noticed that her tummy and her bottom were growing; that meant new t-shirts and jeans. Maybe I could do that next week.

"Okay, Have you prepared everything? Black pot — no, not the non-stick one, don't you know the sadza pot? Find the *mugoti* for mixing, the *mugwagwa* for dishing, a cup of cold water, a jug of boiling water and a cup or saucer to take the mealie meal. Look at Mama. And copy — okay?"

I put a cup of mealie meal into the black pot and stirred with a little water until it was thickish, like porridge. I put the plate on six and stirred in the boiling water.

"You need to keep stirring it until it starts to boil. It must be a bit thick, like this. No pimples." I showed her on my *mugoti* and let the mixture fall back into the pot. Maita did the same. "Right. Now that it's boiling, lid on — twenty minutes."

"All right, Mama — I'm coming back." Maita left.

"*Muri kubika neyi*? What are you eating with the sadza?" Vaida asked, rolling her eyes at Maita's back. "We got some *mukaka* because you know Garikayi loves it. Me and Maita have chicken and tsunga."

"Just beef and veg. Nothing exciting. What's new that side?"

"You remember the businessman — Robson Murewa?" I nodded. "He has three Small Houses and now he's added a twenty-seven-year-old!"

This time I rolled my eyes.

"Isn't he more than sixty now? What is he trying to prove?"

"*Hameno*! This new one —— Rugare, has started a Facebook page for Small Houses to discuss how to handle the Big House."

"Ah ah! The girlfriends want to discuss the wives? What goes on there?"

"Their gang go visit Big House to tell how it's going to work. So, they went… "

"Hello, Mama!"

I love my children, but sometimes they disturb in the middle of juicy, juicy drama.

"Hello, my baby! Where were you all this time?" He was growing up so fast, without me. His skinny knees were covered in dust and his grey khaki shorts had green marks from the grass. A few more items to buy.

"I was playing with Ryan next door. Aunty Viada, why didn't you call me?" He started crying. "Mama, when are you coming to take us to the London?"

"Gari, don't cry. I'll be coming soon. You hear. I have to make lots of money first."

"Mama, it's twenty minutes." Maita was back.

"Okay, Maita turn the fire down. Vai, help her, please." I watched the flames jump up and lick the sides of the pot before Vaida took control. "Five minutes," I repeated to Maita.

"I came first for maths, Mama," Maita said, she must have known that Gari had no news.

"Well done, but you must come first for everything." I said, "next holiday — extra lessons! Now it's time. Bring the mealie meal container nearer to the stove. Be careful, don't let the sadza spit on your hand."

"Mama, you're funny! How can the sadza spit?"

"If the fire's too high it can bubble over the top of the pot and land on your hand. Now pour in a little mealie meal — good, now stir round and round."

"Like this?" As Maita asked, the chair she was standing on shook a little. I reached my hand towards the screen. "Vaida!" She was my ears, tongue and my hands. Even then I couldn't catch my daughter if she fell. It was painful.

"Right. Keep adding a little mealie meal."

"It's getting thicker, Mama."

"It's going to be *mbodza* — I'm not eating that!" Gari stuck his tongue out and pointed his finger down his throat.

"That's not a nice thing to say — Maita, now you must do like this — figure of eight — no, no just your arm not your whole body."

Sissy Vaida and Gari were laughing behind Maita.

"Just a minute… " I had to leave the room. I let tears fall quietly while I stood in the living room.

This is foolish — big women like me shouldn't feel homesick!

I washed my face in the bathroom and went back to the kitchen.

"Okay — I'm back!"

The sadza on both sides of the screen was sighing the way it does when it's been cooked well. This was going to be good, the last bit of the air was forced out. By six o'clock London time and seven o'clock Zim time, the sadza was ready. We sat in front of our phones to continue their conversations. Spotify helped us with Oliver Mutukudzi's Holiday — this was a day for laughing.

We palmed our sadza into round balls then dipped it into the tomato relish and a few green slivers. We ate at

113

the same time. Sweet tomatoey relish and spicy beef with the sour taste of the greens. I sucked the air in — it was good, man! Especially with a little piri-piri.

"And how is the Sadza?" I asked Gari

"It's only okay because Aunty Vaida was here to save the day."

I pretended not to notice Maita kick Gari under the table.

"Mama, she's kicking me."

"You guys can't even stop fighting — just one day a week when you see me like this."

It was quiet after that. But I could see the eyes killing each other across the table. It was better not to see them. After, I watched Vaida pour them each a glass of Mazoe squash. When the children had left, I had a glass of wine. I never used to drink. But this cold weather, the women on television always drinking, sooner or later, I was going to start. It's the culture here.

"So, has their father been?" I asked Vaida, I sipped the red wine. This one was strong.

"Ah no, he sent someone with twenty dollars on Wednesday and said he will come today, but the children are going to bed soon. So *ameno*!"

"Bastard! Who needs him? I have someone better here."

"Don't tell me, sis! Who is he? Where is he from?"

"He's from Nigeria. His name is Okafor. He's coming tomorrow."

"That's nice, sis. What about your friend?"

114

"Which one, now?"

"The Nigerian one, your neighbour."

"Oh, you mean Abi? She's a bit funny these days. I don't know what her problem is. Don't let that man take my children to the village. I know his mother wants to do those rituals. I don't want. I'll be sending for them soon — I don't want them to give me problems when they get here."

"We are going to mother's house tomorrow. We'll come back late just in case he comes."

"Good. I sent with Western Union this morning, so, you can collect on Monday since you won't be there tomorrow. It's cash so be careful where you change it. I don't want to hear stories. *Pa later ka.*"

"Okay, sissy. Thank you. Speak to you next Friday."

By nine, I had phoned everyone and caught up on all the Chinoyi gossip. Time to party. I turned up the music and danced in the centre of the small lounge. At eight thirty, there was a tap, tap on the door — it was Abi.

"My sister, wo. You are really enjoying. Did you leave some saza for me?" Abi asked. She was smiling but her eyebrows remained up as if she was seeing something scary. They reminded me of Miheala from work. I wondered if they went to the same place to get them shaved off and put back with brown paint.

"Yes, there is plenty for you. You didn't need to bring anything." I received the meat dish that she brought. "I have already eaten."

"Oh! You didn't wait for me, wo?"

115

"No, I told you, Abi, on Fridays I eat with my family via WhatsApp. It's as if we are in the same room."

"Oh, I thought you said we were going to eat together, Beauty." Abi's mouth made that funny shape, as if she'd smelt something bad.

"I said that you could come and eat."

"Why did you invite me if you don't want to eat with me?"

"Abi, Fridays I eat with my kids. Sometimes I like to do something that doesn't involve other people."

"Oh, so I am other people? Am I bothering you?"

"Abi, sit down. Let me dish for you."

Abi's phone rang.

"I am here at this, my friend's flat. Where are you?" I knew she must be talking to a man. Her face was all — you know what I mean. She nodded her head. "I'm coming now. No, you wait there. Let me open the door then you'll see me."

She left the door open and came back a few minutes later with a man as black as midnight. The best thing about him was his teeth, so white and straight. I allowed his chunky palm to slide on mine. A bit rough and dry, he must do a job where he has to wash his hands all the time. He wasn't my type — too short. He gave me that look, if Abi wasn't there he would try. I knew then that he's a facey, facey guy.

"I was just about to warm up some food for Abi. Please sit down and eat with her."

"We are not staying for that — you want put juju in my man's food?" Abi said.

I laughed because I thought she was joking but now, I'm not so sure. I closed the door behind Abi and her dark chocolate man, then I kissed my teeth long and hard and laughed and laughed. Wait till she sees my Okafori. Mmm! Now that's a man!

The next morning, I was excited because he was coming to take me out. I had things to prepare. I wondered if he was still as handsome as I remembered. I left for the salon and the nail place before eight and on the way back, I stopped at Lidl to get a few drinks and snacks for Okafor's visit. I was back by eleven, looking sharp. I admired myself in the mirror, front, back, side. Yah! I was looking good. I knew it.

I liked Victoria to do my hair — she knew how to make me look sexy. She had made a weave with one side short and the other long over my left eye. It was a golden-brown colour to go with my light skin. My skin is African — the colour, but a bit light. Lighter than Abi's. Well, yes, I did use skin lightening for some time. But I think this is okay, so I've stopped now. I got out my dress — the one I had been keeping for a day like today — it's a black and white made from shweshwe material. A long one down to my ankles. I like the way the black and white patterns match my white sofa and even the silver on the edge of the coffee table.

I sat on the sofa with my purple sandals resting on the cream rug and leaned against the purple cushions. Just like that — admiring. Then I remembered the silver earrings and put them on.

Then he knocked on the door.

My stomach started doing that dancing thing. You know, when something good is coming.

Phew!

Then I let him in. I watched him come in, hoping that he wouldn't hit his head by the top there, by the door.

"Hello, my dear." His voice was so deep it ran around the room first then came back and hit me right there. I was smiling, maybe a bit too much.

"Okafor, *shah* — you came!"

"Of course. What is *shah*?"

"Friend — it means my friend. Just like that."

"Am I your friend? Really? I will show you that I am more than that."

Well, I had to go to the kitchen to get a drink — he was too much. But I liked it.

"Coffee?" I shouted from the kitchen. I broke a piece of kitchen paper and moped my forehead. I can't remember when I last felt like this.

"Coffee and love taste best when hot!" He said and stood up to prove it when I came back with his coffee.

I was giggling whilst he was telling me all those things, love what-what. I hoped he was a good lover too. In the middle of everything, there was a tap-tap on the door. I was about to get up to open when Abi walked in. After the night before, I was surprised that she came. I suppose she wanted to check out Okafor. Well, let her check.

She wasn't looking her best. But I don't think she knew that the pink lipstick and purple eyeshadow were shouting. Maybe that's what she likes. Or maybe it's the style these days. Who knows? Me, I like just a little on the brush — like that, light touch.

"This is Abi." I was trying to be nice, so was he. He jumped up to greet her and smiled politely.

"Abi — Abiola? Yoruba?"

"Yes," Abi giggled.

Eh eh, was that a curtsey?

"Nice to meet you, Okafor." He smiled. That Abi she kept staring. Just sitting there. I got up to get her a drink and bring the snacks. When I came back in, she looked at me.

"Beauty, where did you get that wig? It's nice!"

I just looked at her. I'm sure it's written in a book somewhere — that is not done. No.

"This is my hair!"

Abi stood up and reached her hand towards my head. I caught her wrist and smacked it like I was killing a mosquito. Abi laughed. But I knew it hurt.

"Ah, I also see that you had your eyelashes done — where did you get them done?"

"Eh?" was all Okafor could say. He coughed.

Serious?

"The bathroom is that way?" Okafor left to give me time and space to sort her out.

"What is wrong with you, Abi?"

"There's nothing wrong — eventually, he'll know that it's all fake." She thought she was being clever.

"Why are you trying to embarrass me?"

"I was just joking," Abi said, she even smiled, like she was saying something nice.

"If you were in such a joking mood, why didn't you just joke about that clown makeup you are wearing."

"Ehh?"

"I think you should leave now."

"It was a joke — I was just... "

"Get out!" I opened the door and shooed her out like a chicken. Then I locked it.

When Okafor returned, it was quiet.

"Has she gone?"

I nodded.

"That's a foolish woman. You must be more careful about how you choose your friends." He massaged my shoulders, I know he felt bad for me. "It is not necessary to blow out the other person's lantern to let yours shine. Let's forget about her and go somewhere nice."

Okafor had a nice, shiny, poshy car parked across the road. When I got in, I couldn't help looking up at the window of Abi's flat. I hoped she was seeing me. Okafor sat in the driver's seat and moved the car smoothly like that — onto the road.

It was beautiful today, lots of sunshine — like home in January. I just hoped it wouldn't rain like it does at home in January. I let the air from the window blow through my weave to keep me cool. For the first few minutes, Okafor concentrated on the road. I admired him by the side of my eye. He had a longish face, with a short beard that came down round his jaw and over the top of his mouth. His colour was a deeper brown than mine — I like dark men. His nose was straight down when you looked at it from the side, but when I was facing him it spread down across like an aeroplane from the top. It pressed against mine when he kissed me with those thick lips. He was tall and wide so that he didn't look too bad standing next to me, because I'm a big girl.

It was quiet — just the tick-ticking of the indicator as Okafor turned the car here and there. I reached over and played with his hair, it was soft and just long enough for me to curl a small piece on my little finger. He smiled at me.

Then, his fingers pressed a few more knobs on the dashboard. The car filled with soft music. Okafor knew all the words. He squeezed my hand.

If it makes any difference
I still love you girl
You're my weakness
You changed my world...
Ah yah! This is romance.

After about an hour, we got to 605 on the Old Kent Road. The restaurant was packed full of people and the smell of fish and strong perfume. One of the waiters recognised Okafor.

"Sir, how are you? And madam? I have a table for you."

We dodged the tables, it was like we were dancing to our table at the back of the room. I was surprised at how quickly they served us. I was tasting Nigerian food for the first time, so I tried the fish and plantain. The fish covered most of a big plate and the plantains and salad were around the edge of the plate like a fan. It was very nice, especially with the hot pepper sauce. Okafor had the assorted goat meat for starters and *edikanikong* with pounded yam.

"What is that?" I asked him.

"It's one of our traditional meals — it's a mixture of meat and vegetables. This pounded yam I've ordered is similar to your saza.

"It's Sadza — there's a 'd'," I laughed.

He tried to say it, but the food was too good. So, I stopped the lecture and we ate. Next, we went to a club in East London where we sat drinking and talking to many of Okafor's friends. We were back by my flat at ten p.m. I always remember that day because that's the day we really started to enjoy.

LUKE
27 MAY

You're up earlier than usual today. Showered, dressed, phone plugged, hoping it's a money day. You remember the twenty on the table, so your first stop is Mags and Fags. The lot goes on provisions. A clean pair of jeans and t-shirt mightn't be a bad thing to have handy for whatever work Andy has for you, so you spend forty minutes at the launderette getting a few changes of clothing cleaned up. You hope the strong sunshine will last long enough to dry them through your bedroom window. You need to spend some more time in the sun to get rid of that pasty colour you used to despise. But, you've more important things right now. You walk back to the flat wondering what time Andy will be coming. It's been a long time since you've felt hopeful — purposeful, productive. At the thought of Andy, you check your phone. Two missed calls. No credit means there is no voicemail.

So, you wait...

... Every ten minutes, you check your phone to make sure the signal is still strong. At nine-thirty, you decide that you'll risk leaving your phone on charge to buy some more credit from Mags and Fags. Your flat door is open when you get back. You know that no self-respecting burglar would want to break into your flat.

"Hello… hello""

You even check the bathroom. No Andy. You slump on the sofa, phone in hand, wondering what to do next. No new messages have come in. Maybe Andy's found someone else to work for him. Someone that's always available. It must be worth one more try. When you dial the number, the ring's got an eerie echo, you realise that it's his phone ringing — he must be close by.

You get off the sofa to meet him. He's short and skinny but his energy fills the small entrance. Your stomach flutters. He wears a navy-blue baker's boy cap pulled over his brows and a Burberry beige and blue shirt open over a white t-shirt and jeans.

"See, now I'm wondering if you're the right man for the job," he says, jabbing a finger. It stings in the pit of your stomach.

"I tried ringing you back. I… "

"Here we go with the excuses. Let's fuckin' hear it then."

"I left my phone charging, see it's an old phone. It takes ages to charge. But… "

"Jesus, fuckin' Chris'! You're just what they're looking for on Jeremy. Muppet. Get it sorted. Yeah? I've given that job to someone else now. That's fifty quid you can't have."

"Haven't you got anything else?"

"No, mate, I don't." He turns to leave then turns back. You can't keep the joy off your face. "I'll tell you what, mate — I do need something doing. Mate of mine needs storage. There. You can earn yourself thirty quid just to bring the stuff here. Twenty to store it, ten to carry it, yeah?"

"You want it doing now?"

"Yeah, of course, it needs fuckin' doing now." You ignore his sarcasm already calculating what that'll buy for Charlotte.

You follow him to a local white goods shop. The length of the walls on either side are burdened. You read the labels; Samsung, Hotpoint, Beko. The floor is grubby with dried, muddy footprints. The place reeks of gas made worse by the heat. Andy nods at someone at the back. He stops testing the small fridge and comes over. He drops a spanner on top of a stove and struggles forward, squeezing between the appliances. He's built like a fridge.

"This is the guy. Just give him one of those trolley things — he'll take it away." Then to you, "Make sure you bring the trolley thing back. Otherwise, you'll have Brian here charging you hire fees." He laughs at his own joke and you notice the black teeth at the back, for the first time. He smooths the hair on the top of his head down, but it springs back into its gelled-back style. You sniff and wipe your nose with the back of your hand. You try not to remember when you used to buy gel and shit. Now the most you can afford is a little lynx for your shower days.

Brian is behind you on the way back. He watches your struggle with the street door then barges in behind you, almost knocking over an old geezer on his way out. The manners of some people. Brian fits the washing machine while you stand feeling out of place in your own kitchen doorway. You want to ask if you can use it, but you don't. You push the trolley back to the shop. Andy is at the back swearing at someone on his mobile.

"Stupid cunt." When he finishes, he tries to use his anger to intimidate you. But you still ask.

"Andy. You said thirty quid."

"I only have twenty here. I'll give you the other ten next time."

You're not sure if you imagined the look he gives Brian. You're a bit annoyed yet grateful, so you miss the games that Andy is playing with your money situation. The original fifty quid would have been so much better. But at least this has been quickly earned.

"Anything else, boss?" you ask.

You want to laugh at him when he draws himself upwards and sticks his chest out. He looks up at your face.

"Nah, that's it for now. Let's go back to yours. Later, Brian!"

As soon as you get in.

"Where'd he put it? — There. Got it plugged in? You can use it now and again — not too much mind. Just to keep it working."

"You sure he wouldn't mind?"

"Nah — wash those curtains for starters. They're minging."

You can smell the shit coming out of his mouth — but you need the money. So, you think about Charlotte. About the last time you saw her, then you roll a cigarette to blank him out. You look up, he's still fiddling with the back of the machine.

"How long do I need to keep it?"

Andy continues to fuck about with the machine. You listen to the voices from outside as they pass your open windows. While you think about your situation, you roll up more cigarettes and lay them neatly in a small, empty sweet tin. The picture of a couple holding hands in the street across the front distracts and reminds you of Charlotte's mother. They look happy, like the two of you once were.

Andy slides his feet back onto the ground and raises himself before turning around. He sits opposite and fishes a see-through packet out of his jean pocket. It contains crushed brown leaves. You recognise the marijuana, but there's something different about this.

"This stuff is supposed to be lethal." You watch him sniffing in the drug deeply. "Have a drag?" He continues swinging the packet in your direction. He rolls a pinch in tobacco paper and lights it. The thick, grey smoke surges forward from his nostrils. You hate the stink and the fact that it will be around for days.

You light a roll-up and inhale deeply. Your narrow eyes remain focused on Andy. Nicotine and booze are your thing. Familiar satisfaction and highs.

"Y' look shit-scared."

"I'm not fucking scared — of what?"

He looks at the corner and notices your blue and white scarf drying on the clothes thingy.

"QPR?"

You nod.

"You?"

"Blinding fucking game last week."

"Only just — muppet kept taking dives all over the place." At least you support the same football team, that's gotta count for something.

"Watkins? Absolute bollocks! Shit ref. But still 3-1."

You get up and pour a neat vodka. Andy grabs the glass tipping the contents down his throat. He laughs at the look on your face. He offers the last couple of drags of his smoke.

"Next time."

"Any food?"

Without waiting, he opens and slams shut several cupboard doors before grabbing a tin of baked beans. He pours all of it on two slices of fresh toast. That tin was meant to be your supper. Now, you'll have to break a ten to buy another tin. You watch Andy scoff the lot. Finally, he stands near the door.

"When's the next job?"

"Depends — what are you willing to do?"

"What you mean?"

"What if I told you I could pay you five hundred pounds a week? For two days work?"

"I don't want to do anything illegal or nothing like that."

"See, that's your problem, you need to expand your horizons. I can guarantee you protection. Nobody would know, unless you told them."

"I'll have to think about it." You don't trust Andy.

Tight as a fuckin' ducks arse, you think to yourself as he waffles on. You miss the first part of what he's saying and only hear,

"...Or maybe you like pissin' about in this shit hole," he sneers, then leaves.

When you get up to close and lock the door behind him, you discover a letter jammed between the door and the mat that has been pressed further and further down each time the door has been opened. It's from the Department of Works and Pension and it's marked urgent.

The next day you go to the address on the letter for your three o'clock appointment. They've totally fucked things up this time. You need it sorted, or there'll be no benefits. You arrive fifteen minutes early and wait in the waiting area with at least forty other people. The room is stuffy, and the air vibrates and buzzes with people chattering. Some nutter's kicking off at the desk. You wonder if he's got the same problem.

Your name is called, and you step into a small, modern office. The room is bare except for a desk, two chairs, a desktop and a balding, middle-aged man with a grey goatee. He adjusts his rimless glasses as you go in, and he shifts his position. He tries to look professional. You wonder if he's one of the plonkers who's fucked up. He points at the chair opposite him, and you move it outwards by sliding your bottom back, so you can avoid his feet touching yours.

He confirms your details and inks your fingers to have them assigned to your profile.

"You'll get your benefits reinstated in two weeks, there's been a slight mess up. No more than two weeks wait."

"Thanks," you say, standing and wiping the ink onto the leg of your jeans.

Two weeks later you receive a text message saying that your benefits will be reinstated in two weeks time.

That's another promise to Charlotte that I can't keep.

You kick off at the offices and are taken to a room at the back of the building. A dark-haired man sits behind a desk. He looks like a regular at the tanning bar, but you admire how good it looks. His blue eyes sting yours as you sit opposite him.

"Can you confirm your date of birth, full names and full postal address, please?"

After you give him the information, you wait and when he shuffles more papers around and clicks on the computer, you really get pissed off.

"What's going on? Hey look here — not at the fuckin' screen, I'm asking you a question — here, here." You click your fingers at him.

He looks up.

"I'm really sorry about this. We have to straighten things out. It'll take a couple of weeks… "

"Weeks — it's not my bloody fault. You people fucked up."

"I'd ask you not to use that language. And kicking-off won't help. Why don't you just calm down. We're sorting this as fast as we can."

You ball your fist. Then stand up and thump it on the desk. Then leave before he can read you the riot act. Back outside in the sunshine, you shiver. You have exactly ten pounds left.

Fuck!

You start the long walk home.

ABI
2 JULY

Ehe, that Beauty, she wants to come and boss me around. I've been here longer than her, praise God! She can't tell me what to do, wo. I know that if I tell Nurse Katie that she is being difficult, I'm sure she will understand. She can partner me with someone else.

I knocked gently on the office door because I could see that Nurse Katie was busy with the diary and answering the phone.

I don't know if that was what made her refuse to pair me with someone else.

"I thought you two were besties. What happened?"

"N noth… "

"Look, I can't afford to have people who don't get along — I'm not having it." The phone rang, and I thought about how I could change her mind when she came off the phone. She started playing with her hair, wo.

"It's not that I don't get along with Beauty. Actually, I like her a lot — it's just that… " I stood up and closed the office door to give me time to think what I should say.

"Com' on, Abi, spit it out. I haven't got all day."

"Well, the other day, I was just passing Mrs Jones' doorway, and I saw Beauty… "

The emergency bell rang, maybe it was God stopping me from telling a lie. Nurse Katie almost knocked me over when she rushed to the door.

"We'll finish this later… "

BEAUTY

I heard the emergency bell. Lucky I was already in the corridor but me, I was struggling against my thighs but I managed to move fast. I slowed a little so that I could hear a bit about what Nurse Katie was saying, but I couldn't stop to see if it was Abi she was talking to. There were about six other carers telling me to hurry up. The corridors are small — it's only the slim ones that can walk two-two like that. There was shouting from the stairs.

"Come on, Beauty, move — it's probably Mr Davidson again."

Couldn't Nurse Katie see that I couldn't run any faster?

Mr Davidson was up there, over his head. I mean he was angry. Granny Joyce was stuck in the corner in the upstairs lounge. We call her granny because she's so old she should be at home looking after her grandchildren not working as a carer. The television playing Everybody Loves Raymond. Some of them were watching Raymond's dad, Frank, arguing with his wife, Marie —

asking her to stop bossing him around. Mr Davidson must have heard the TV. Mr Davidson removed his trouser belt.

"I told you to leave me alone!" Mr Davidson shouted. Ah ah! No one was even talking to him.

The four residents eating breakfast got up to watch the bioscope. I mean the filim, as they say here.

"Stop it! Frank — Mr Davidson, just calm down," Granny Joyce shouted.

I saw her looking here and there to find where to run. The sofa was on her left, a small coffee table to her right and Mr Davidson in front of her, in the space between the furniture. If she was younger she could have jumped. I didn't want to say anything because, me also, I couldn't jump.

The other carers tried to call Mr Davidson and others were telling him his wife was on the phone. Nurse Katie pointed at the table on the right and one of the carers moved it back. Granny Joyce didn't see the table moved, but Mr Davidson saw it. He moved to the space so that Granny Joyce couldn't go there. Then he flicked his belt. It hit Granny Joyce on the arm, lucky it wasn't the other side with the metal.

"Aww! That really hurt, Mr Davidson. Stop that right now." Granny Joyce was getting mad also.

Mr Davidson started to get more excited and he walked nearer to Granny. I'm sure she was thinking that she won't see her new grandchild who's due anytime. Maybe she was thinking why she didn't retire like other grannies. I felt sorry for her — she grabbed a cushion from the sofa and put it in front of her. Mr Davidson ran towards her and grabbed the cushion. Well, he wasn't really running but he was moving so fast, I thought he was going to fall. He's had so many falls this month because of this type of behaviour. Granny Joyce was pulling the cushion and shouting that he should let go. He was making these funny noises and also shouting.

One of the other carers went and grabbed the belt from Mr Davidson's hand and then she moved back quickly when he turned to her. But, still he was holding onto the cushion. Granny Joyce let go and tried to move that side. Mr Davidson became more angry. Maybe because he didn't have his belt. He went up to Granny and punched her in the face.

"Ohh!" everybody screamed.

Now, I know that Granny Joyce is tough. She was standing there with one hand over her eye and with the other she grabbed another cushion. Nurse Katie tried to talk to Mr Davidson, then I think she thought maybe she should give him an injection, so she went downstairs. Me, I thought it was better to do something more to help Granny Joyce. It was getting late also. Quarter to nine and we hadn't started the washes yet. We didn't have time for this nonsense.

While Mr Davidson was watching Joyce, I walked softly-softly behind him. Then I hugged him from behind. He couldn't move and I could see his neck getting red. He was shouting so loud using bad words. But I couldn't let go. I walked with him backwards until we were near a big chair. I had to talk soft-soft.

"It's okay, Mr Davidson. Don't worry — look they're taking her away."

The other carers were shouting, 'well done, Beauty!' and, 'Beauty saved the day!' I could tell that they were happy they weren't involved, like me and Granny Joyce. They just left me with Mr Davidson. Nurse Katie came back with the injection. She stood watching, wondering what to do next.

"Look it's just us here. It's going to be okay. Shall we call Mrs Davidson — Marj? Let's see what time she's coming," I asked Mr Davidson.

I made him some toast and everywhere I turned, I could just see that Abi, like she was checking me. I wasn't sure but I thought I saw her go there by Mrs Jones's room.

ABI

"Mrs Jones — wake up!" She wouldn't wake up. She was just squeezing her eyes. While she was facing the wall, I closed the door. She just made me angry, ignoring me. Then I thought about Beauty, always showing off and trying to pretend she was better than everybody.

At first, I just wanted to wake Mrs Jones up. You know maybe just a squeeze. I put my hands under the duvet and grabbed her tummy. I just twisted a bit, not much. She moved but didn't wake up. I thought maybe I should just do small, small like that again. That time she woke up.

"Aww — stop it! Stop it! you're hurting me." I had to jump back because she tried to hit me.

"Shh, shh." I turned the television loud. And I checked the door.

"Who is that? Stop it, you wicked witch — you're hurting me. Stop it." Listen to her calling me a witch, I bet if it was Beauty, she wouldn't say that.

"I'm not doing anything to you, settle down. It's me, Beauty."

"Leave me alone, Beauty."

I didn't plan it, it just happened. Then I got scared, I checked the corridor then I went quickly into the linen room to get towels. I went to wash another resident. Next thing I heard people running up and down the corridor and then I met Nurse Katie going into Mrs Jones's room. I listened from the corridor.

"Mrs Jones — do you know what happened?"

"It was Beauty."

"How do you know? Did you see her?"

"Beauty, Beauty — she told me."

Nurse Katie came out.

"It couldn't have been Beauty — she was upstairs with Mr Davidson. She's only just finished with him."

BEAUTY

I was just finished there with Mr Davidson when Nurse Katie called me to the office. I thought she was calling me to say thank you, Beauty, what-what. Instead I was told to stay away from Mrs Jones's room. Ah ah!

I showed Nurse Katie the allocation book. I hadn't worked with Mrs Jones for the past two weeks. I had spent all morning with Mr Davidson, when did I have time to damage that woman?

Unfortunately, Mrs Jones's daughter came that day. I stood outside the office to listen. I know Nurse Katie knew I was there because she left the door open.

"Margaret, Please, come to my office." Nurse Katie offered a cup of tea to Mrs Jones's daughter.

"I really would like to spend time with my mother, rather than sit here drinking tea. She's upset."

"I have a duty to notify you that your mother has some fresh bruises on her abdomen. I'm just looking into how she could possibly have got them. My carers are extra careful with the residents."

"Mother tells me that somebody called Beauty did something to her. I can't make out what she's saying because she's so upset." I nearly fainted when she said that. When did I do that?

"Well, that's what she says. But we have evidence that Beauty was elsewhere this morning."

"My mother is not in the habit of telling lies."

"I'm sorry, that's not what I intended to say — it's just that I think that your mum might have gotten the names confused."

"Now, you think that she has dementia? You're not a doctor. What right do you have to diagnose people? You're not a bloody doctor, are you?"

"I'm sorry, Margaret, but I think you misunderstand... "

"It's you that misunderstands — I don't want that Beauty near my mother. And if I don't get some answers, I'll be calling the CQC."

When I heard her coming out, I quickly went the other way. Then I went in to see Nurse Katie. Next thing, safe-guarding was involved and the manager said that I should leave early. I went to the staffroom to get my things and go home. Abi was sitting in the staffroom having tea and bread.

"Oh, Beauty, are you leaving us? We've still got a few hours of the shift left... "

I thought it was better to be quiet, because I could smack her and make things worse. As I was closing the door, I heard her talking loudly.

"You can't trust anybody... "

Abi? I'll catch up with her later.

LUKE
1 JUNE

You're well and truly fucked. This is the time you'd be chain-smoking if only you could afford it, instead you take it easy on the small parcel of bacie left. The dried crust of bread suddenly looks tempting. You gobble it with black, sugarless tea, and try not to wretch. You think about calling Andy, but you don't want to appear desperate.

Outside you see a guy in Burberry, the same height as him crossing the road. You rush outside in time to see him get into the passenger seat of a vehicle as it speeds off. He turns towards you — it's not Andy.

You finger your phone.

"Hi Mum... "

"Luke!"

You hear a man's voice in the background asking her what you want.

"He's my son," then to you, "You all right?"

"Not really, Mum. The benefits office has messed up and... "

"Oh, Lukey, you still haven't got a job? Darlin', I told you to get it sorted."

The man's voice growls close to the phone, "Useless fuckin' muppet, told you he wanted something."

"Who else is he expected to turn to?"

The argument continues between them. There's shouting, you hear something crash — glass shattering, then a door slam.

"Mum, Mum — are you okay?"

Shit! I knew I shouldn't have called.

The man's voice is muffled, menacing.

"Lukey, I'll send you a little — but you have to promise not to call for a while. I'll call you, okay? All I got is forty. I've got to go now."

"Mum, are you going to be all right? I mean he's not hitting you or anything?"

"It's all right — don't call — I'll call you tomorrow when he's gone to work. 'Bye. 'Bye."

You sit tight and wait. Mum calls later for five minutes when her bloke's out to the off-licence and tells you to expect the money. You suggest that she move back into the flat with you, but she says he's not a bad bloke really. It sounds worse than it is and she can handle him. She sends the money wrapped in kitchen foil. She's added another fiver.

☐ Beans,
☐ Eggs,
☐ Oven chips,
☐ Bread,
☐ Tea bags,

☐Milk,
☐Sugar
from Lidl
and bacie from Mags and Fags.

At least the weather's good, so you walk back slowly. On an impulse, you spend a few minutes in front of Tescott's odd-job notice board. Every little detail gets your attention. Nothing.

You finger the thirty in your pocket. It's a nice day for the park — with Charlotte.

You quicken your step as you see one of your neighbours holding the street door open with their big shop. She looks knackered so you offer to carry the groceries up when you notice her belly.

"Pablo at work then?"

"He's in Spain."

You help her with her bags. She reads your mind and slips you something. You slide the fiver against your small stash in your pocket. It's awkward for a minute.

"Later."

You take the stairs two-at-a-time down to your gaff. The door's open. You can only hope. You try to be casual. So, you stop for a second outside the door, then stroll in. You shouldn't have bothered. You sit on the couch and try to think of something.

The next thing you know, you're back at the Benefits office. The visit starts pleasantly enough with you enquiring about their progress with your case.

"You have all the energy to come down here, why don't you check our website for a job?" The woman's trying to give advice and that. When you get back from the lav — she has her back to you, her voice is loud.

"… just fed up. Take that lad, nothing wrong with him except he's too lazy to go out and get a job. I'm glad they messed up his paperwork, means he can go out and look for a fricking job like the rest of us. His whole family's probably on benefits — frickin' waste of space."

"Oh yeah?" You're moving towards her. "Who do you think you fuckin' are? Judging me and my family like that?"

She swings round, her eyes large. She backs away. Her colleague comes between you.

"Now, just settle down. She wasn't talking about you."

"Think you're hard?" You're eyeball to eyeball. He doesn't blink.

"If you don't go back to your seat, we'll have you thrown out."

"Yeah? Oh? I'm shaking with fear."

She slips away.

"First you lose my fuckin' documents. Then you insult me."

"Look, if you just calm down, I could look into it for you."

"I'm tired of waiting while you look into it. It's been weeks and fuck all's the result. So, don't you fuckin' tell me to calm down."

Someone touches your arm from behind. You take a swing at them. You find yourself on the floor with your arms pinned down. You're grateful when the police come and cuff you to take you down to the station.

"The joke's on you — I'm going to get free board and lodging." You realise how stupid that sounds after you've said it.

The policeman looks at you pityingly.

"Mind your head." He pushes your head down as he guides you into the back seat. In ten minutes, you're at the station. He takes your prints, but asks you to an office in the back.

"I've got a lad about same age as you. Twenty?" You look back at him without admitting to being twenty-two. "I'd hate for him to get a record just because he got a little upset. It'll only make it harder for you to get a job in future. I know that it's already pretty hard as it is. Now, I'm prepared to go in and talk to them about dropping charges, after all, you didn't actually hit someone. But you have to promise you'll apologise and not go in again until they've sorted everything out for you."

As you stare at the wall, the fight starts to leave you and you realise that you're scared shitless. A criminal record will scar you for life, nobody employs a crim. You know things would get even tougher than they are now. You meet the copper's eye and nod.

It works out. You don't want to go home but you do and meet the pregnant woman again. You nod at her,

"All right?"

144

She nods back and stops.

"Want to talk?"

You sit on the bench, under the tree in the green. She sits beside you and offers you a smoothie in a kiddies carton.

"When's the baby due?"

"Five months."

"So, how comes Pablo's in Spain?"

"Ah, you know how these things are... "

You nod, even though you don't.

"I have a daughter. I'd give my right arm to spend the day with her."

"It's always complicated."

She tells you about missing her family in Brazil and that she'll probably move back there for childcare. She asks about your family and you mention Mum, without giving too much detail. Somehow, the episode at the benefits office makes its way into the conversation. Of course, you leave some stuff out.

"Would you like me to ask at my work? We might be able to get something for you. Nothing much, maybe some admin, part-time something like that?"

You rub your thigh enthusiastically and nod.

"Mind you, I can't promise nothing."

You're on a promise from Andy, benefits and now this. You sit quietly for a while.

"Thanks for the smoothie, I've just seen someone I need to talk to."

She looks over at Andy and back at you. She raises her hand at you.

"I'll leave a note under your door if there's anything."

"Thanks."

BETTY
1 JULY

The last few days have been a flurry of activity. It all started when the nurses visited. Imagine two of them turning up like that in one day. That Schoo — oh, I can't remember her name. it was a funny one it reminded me of Scholls. I remember when those shoes first come out in the seventies, I think it was, and they said they were good for your feet. Well, they were damned uncomfortable — maybe that was the point. I mean the way they worked.

Wonder when the chiropodist's coming. My toenails need seeing to. Wonder if she'd be up to putting a splash of colour on my toes to cheer me up. The carpet's had a right old clean. Someone organised for the cleaner to come in and give the flat a good going-over. Can't barely recognise it. Mind you, I take exception to being bossed around in me own flat. That takes the biscuit. It really does.

That social worker's due. When did she say she's coming? Better check the calendar. I think she wrote it down. There's nothing to do but sit and wait. That's all I seem to do these days — sit and wait. I feel the tears working their way out. We' ll have none of that today. The carer's been and helped me to have a shower, my hair's dry, and I managed to get some face powder on and a little lippy. She suggested eyeshadow — but that's where I drew the line. I'm not trying to give Bozo the clown a run for his money. Anyway, it's not as if I'm going anywhere. I can't remember the last time I went out, haven't been past my own front door for far too bleeding long. Wonder what it would feel like to be outside and feel the wind blowing on my cheeks.

Mind you, I don't think I'd be able to walk that far. It's no good getting a wheelchair either, who would bleeding push it? Last time I checked I had three able-bodied grandchildren. Expect they've got better things to do than come here.

There's the intercom, again. I hope it's someone nice again. If I just shuffle quickly...

I'm halfway to the door when I remember they've put the key safe in. I'm not sure how I feel about that — I mean, every bleeding person, carer and his dog will be able to just walk in here without my say-so. And what if I'm on the lav? No bleeding dignity when you get old.

I just make it back to my chair when there's a knock on the door. At least this one's got manners.

"Come in!" I hear the key in the lock and in walks this girl. No uniform, mind. Wonder if they know she's working without a uniform?

"Hello, Mrs Lyons, do you remember me? I'm Mukai, the social worker. I came to see you the other day."

As she gets closer, I remember seeing her. Has it been a few days already? That's the problem with just sitting here day and night, they just seem to merge into this big blob of daylight and sleeping. Mind you, I've been doing a lot of that lately — sleeping. They must think I'm lazy - fat cow. But I really enjoy sleeping — Harry's always there and I don't feel so lonely. Oh Harry...

"... would it be all right if I come in and talk to you?"

She's been talking and my mind had wandered off. I nod and point to the sofa, it's near enough for me to get a good look at her. This one's slim and muscly, not like the other one who looked like she'd not had a decent meal for weeks. This one has a big afro — it's all tinsely and shiny, how much oil did she have to use to get it like that? Someone once told me they use coconut oil in their hair. Fancy that, putting oil in your hair? The minute mine gets oily, I like to shampoo it. Still, it's not something I think about these days. What do I think about? Can't bleeding remember most of the time.

"I came to find out how you're finding the support you're getting?"

"Everyone's very nice and helpful, thank you." Now I remember, she came with about a hundred forms. And she spent hours asking me questions. I wonder if she's managed to find my Angela. She carries on talking but I'm not in a listening mood today. Must say, she speaks very good English — at least I can understand her. I wonder if she was born here. Perhaps I'll ask her. She's very dark though — I mean there's not much difference between her complexion and the black cat we used to have years ago. Surely, if she was British, she'd be a few shades lighter, not being funny or nothing — but if she was born here, she wouldn't have had to toil in the black African hot sun. I never really noticed beauty in these people before. But she is quite stunning. Her skin is even all over and she has those cheekbones that we all wanted when I was younger. Lovely big eyes, brown I think they are. I wonder if she has a fella. But I don't envy her those thick lips, they must get in the way of things. They're just too big for comfort.

"Do you have any questions?" she asks me, her voice is gentle, and she looks concerned.

I did have a question, but now I can't remember what it was. I stare back at her.

"Are you feeling all right?"

"Yes, yes, I'm fine. Could do with a cup of tea."

She gets up to make it and, as she walks past me, I get a whiff of her perfume. I can't make it out — it's flowery but not that cheap kind of overpowering smell. It reminds me of my niece, Ann. She took me out for the day once and we spent ages in House of Fraser trying on all those perfumes and she liked one similar to this. Then we went and had tea at the Savoy down the West End, pretending we was posh and that. It must have cost her a packet. She said I was worth every penny. Then she had to marry a bloke from America and move out there — California. Plenty of good blokes round here. She could have found herself an English lad and stayed closer to home. I suppose I should be content with the Christmas cards with American dollars. Last time I checked, there was five hundred dollars. Maybe this one can change it for me and put it in my account. That is, if Angela hasn't made off with it.

Oh, she's coming back. Did I say she could go riffling in my biscuit tin? I don't remember hearing the water running. Did she wash her hands?

"I hope you don't mind, I washed my hands in the sink."

What? Is she a bleeding mind-reader too?

"Has the carer been coming three times a day?"

"She's been coming once a day. I think. I don't remember if she came yesterday."

"Oh, I see. I'll check with the agency. If you have any problems, will you remember to call me?"

"What sort of problems?" Why send carers if you think they'll be a problem?

I suddenly notice how tall she is. Very elegant. Maybe she should be in a magazine modelling clothes. But do they use dark people like these in the magazines? I can't say I've seen them. She must be the darkest person I've ever met.

"Do you have any questions? Or anything that's bothering you?"

Now I remember what I wanted to ask her.

"Were you born here?" I see her demeanour change. That's not a rude question is it?

"I meant questions about the service we are offering. If you must know — no, I was born in Zimbabwe."

There I told you, we don't have people like that here.

"Well, if there's nothing else… ?"

She waits a moment, all poised with her breasts pointing out as if they're accusing me. I stare back at her and envy the tiny waist, mind, that bottom's too big. I expect she can't help it.

"I'll be in touch in a month or so. Here is the number of the care agency in case the carer doesn't turn up or anything like that. 'Bye."

I nod and half-smile. Then she floats towards the door and closes it gently behind her, leaving her perfume dancing around the room.

PABLO
JULY

It had been a few weeks since the fight with the short guy who tried to cheat Sanjay. I couldn't be sure, but I thought I saw him hanging around the block. On one occasion, he seemed to be coming from the ground floor out of Luke's flat. I meant to follow it up, but so many things were happening at once and I hardly had time for anything else. It could be someone else.

Cecilia was pregnant. I was excited. At first.

Then on Cecilia's birthday. I went to surprise her at work. When I arrived, she was attending a client meeting at the client's office in Leicester. Her phone went to voicemail and I left her message. I was bored so I went to the Elixir to kill the time. I ended up serving and earned a little overtime. Elixir reminded me of university — fun with integrated stress.

Cecilia called back just after nine p.m.

"Where are you?" She sounded flushed — can you say that about the way a person sounds?

"I'm at work — are you back in London?" I thought I could hear someone in the background. "How come you didn't tell me that you were going out of town?"

"The client called after I arrived at work."

"When are you getting home?"

"Ah, sorry, Pablo, did you have something planned for my birthday?" When I sighed into the phone, she continued, "I won't be back until tomorrow — we have some urgent stuff to complete."

For some reason, over the past few months, I preferred the thought of her to actually being with her, but that day I was absolutely gutted. We had never celebrated birthdays apart ever since we had moved in together.

"I guess you have to do what you have to."

"Sorry... I... "

"'Bye."

I went home to wallow in pity and loneliness. That's the day I saw that guy coming out of the block. He seemed to see me and then change direction. I felt pleased, he knew not to mess with me. I had other things to occupy my thoughts — like what was really going on with Cecilia?

I didn't mean to spy on her, but I found myself in a café across the street from her office late one afternoon. I saw her leave the building and stand outside the door around six. Then this woman arrived, she smiled up at her and they walked in the opposite direction.

When I called her number, she took the phone out, checked the screen, then put it back in her bag. They continued walking then disappeared into the underground. Maybe she was with a client and they were discussing something important. I went home and fixed dinner. She walked in at eight.

"I called you today."

"It's hard to take calls when I'm at work."

The wine tasted metallic.

"I couldn't wait anymore — besides I can't keep warming it... "

The potatoes felt like cotton wool, I forced them down with a gulp of wine.

"How was work?"

I sawed the beef.

"Quiet — left early." I pushed the plate away.

"What's really going on with you?"

"Nothing, just work."

And that's where we were, stuck in this place between heaven and hell. In that moment I thought about Brazil, the little house in Granada, the baby.

"I'm going to see my parents. Alone."

She looked hurt when I said that, I looked away.

"How long for?" Her voice soft and broken. I felt pleased.

"Two weeks. Maybe longer if they can spare me at the bar."

"Maybe I could come and join you — just for a few days."

"No, you stay here."

"But... "

"You're always at work anyway. You won't notice."

"When?"

"Tomorrow."

For once, I refused her. I turned over. The next morning, I took a small suitcase to Heathrow and bought the first ticket to Malaga. I phoned my brother, Alejandro, to meet me at the airport and we took the two-hour drive to Granada. Then further south to Cherin. The olive groves welcomed me home. For the first few days, I felt I was a boy again in my parents' house — waking up early to help with harvesting and staying out all night to drink copious amounts of beer in the shelter amongst the olives. On Sundays after church, the family would set the table on the veranda and eat premade tapas of olives, tortilla, pescaito fritos, jambon de Trevelez. Our glasses were constantly replenished with Riojo. When it grew dark, I went inside to help mama prepare the papas a lo pobre. I love to watch mama slice the potatoes and peppers

I woke up one morning and decided I wasn't ready to go back. Cecilia had phoned me once — It had been an odd conversation, it ended too soon when Mama called me to eat. That weekend, me and Alejandro drove down to the coast. I had always dreamt of taking Cecilia, but it no longer felt right. I smiled at Alejandro, when had he grown out of the little shit that couldn't keep a secret?

After three weeks, I told Cecilia I'd be back at the end of August maybe September in time for the new uni year.

"I could use your help now." She called me a few days later via WhatsApp as she wanted me to see how big she'd grown.

"I'll be there soon — before you go on maternity leave."

"I need you now."

"I've just got some family stuff to take care of. As soon as I finish, I'll be on the next plane."

"Family? What stuff? Your family's here with me. Me and your baby."

We argued back and forth and fortunately, the network cut out. Alejandro caught me just outside my room.

"Why don't you go to her?"

"I just need to be here."

"Isn't she having your baby?"

I hesitated too long. He opened his mouth to say something.

"I don't want to talk about it."

We didn't go on any more trips after that. I hung around the homestead and, when I felt like it, I went to pick olives and muck around with the workers. I had my eye on Sylvera — we'd grown up together and I'd always avoided her because she felt like a sister. My years away had broken the bond.

One night we crept into the barn and lay on a blanket on top of the hay. I could feel the expectation radiating from her. Having one baby on the way slowed my reaction. She reached over and caressed my face, then she kissed me deeply. I felt obliged to make love to her.

Afterwards, neither of us spoke. I was scared of what she might expect from me.

She sighed, got up and dressed in the moonlight. Without a word, she left. I knew, then, it was time to go

157

back to England. I'd hopefully get my old job back and see if I still felt like being with Cecilia. I went indoors to wash for supper. Mama wasn't in the kitchen as usual. I found her on the front porch with a bizarre expression on her face, her body slouched to one side. Alejandro and I followed the ambulance to the hospital. We left a message for Papa to meet us there.

LUKE
JUNE

For once Andy keeps his promise and arrives shortly before nine p.m.

"Driver's licence?"

You pull it out of your wallet.

"What am I, a fuckin' traffic cop?"

You shove it back in your pocket. He looks thuggish, sinister-like today. You eye his skinny leather jeans with zips on the front, follow the legs downwards to where they are tucked into black combat boots. Inside his leather jacket is a black t-shirt. The weather's cooler and rainy today, but it's still a ridiculous get-up for summer.

"Follow me."

You trail behind to the parking space at the back. He stops next to a bronze Honda Civic. The windows are open and you notice a young boy sitting in the passenger seat.

"I need you to take Alex to Manchester. Alex'll direct you once you get there."

"What's in Manchester?"

"Alex has a few deliveries to make. Don't you Alex?"

Alex stops fiddling with the radio, and looks up. Either Alex is a very pretty boy or a tomboy.

Andy hands you fifty for fuel.

"Be back by tomorrow. Bell me when you get in. Alex knows what to do."

You know you ought to find out about the deliveries, but it seems harmless enough. You imagine you're taking your little brother or sister to Manchester. Behind the wheel, you punch in Manchester city centre into the satnav. Alex turns the volume up on the radio and you're off.

On the way out of London, the North Circular is chocka. When you hit the M6 the traffic begins to flow a lot easier the further up you drive. You start to relax and speed up a little, the needle nudges seventy-five.

"Stay at seventy." You're decided Alex is a girl, after all. "Don't want to be stopped for speeding. That could lead to a search — you know what that would mean?"

"What would it mean, then? What's the parcels we're carrying?"

"If the boss didn't see fit to tell you — who am I to say?"

"How old are you anyway?"

"Old enough." She lights a cigarette, her hands are tiny, maybe fourteen-year-old hands.

"Where do you go to school then? Do your parents…"

"From social services then? Fuckin' questions, questions everyone wants to know… "

"Okay, just calm down. Was just chattin,' that's all."

"I don't need besties. Just keep driving and I'll tell you when we get there."

You're now even more curious about Alex and take in the dirty clothes and matted unwashed hair — an odd combination with the red Nike junior MX, the last time you saw them, they were a hundred quid. You wonder when she last had a good bath, the atmosphere in the car is positively minging. You start to think maybe this trip wasn't such a good idea. But it's too late now and besides, a little cash would go a long way to helping your food situation.

Four hours is a long time to just drive and listen to the suggestive rap spewing out of the speakers. You don't need more agro from the passenger seat, so you concentrate on the drive. For most of it, you wonder how many trips you can do each week and how much stuff you can get Charlotte. You might even be able to afford an old banger to make it easier to visit her.

When you arrive on the outskirts of Manchester, Alex sits up and directs you into Cheetham Hill Road. She signals for you to pull over.

"Wait here."

She pulls a rucksack from beneath the seat and removes a brown package which she fits under the waistband of her black tracksuit bottoms. You're here now, so you go with the flow.

You watch her disappear into a house with thick curtains and dirty windows. You could be anywhere in England. She emerges some twenty minutes later — you see her put something black into her waistband and half-walk-half-run back to the car.

"Let's go — hurry up… "

You start the engine and slide the car back onto the road. In the rear-view mirror, you see someone run through the little gate from the house where Alex was and turn down an alley next to the house.

"Everything all right?" you ask Alex, as she switches her yellow hoodie for a blue one.

"Even if it's not, what the fuck do you think you can do about it? You don't even have a fuckin' piece — do you? Wouldn't know how to use it."

She looks up at you.

"Just drive."

You follow her directions to what was once an old pub. The barricade that had sealed the door has been lifted and you see someone come out as the car approaches.

"Leave the engine running, turn the car around to face the way we came. If you don't see me come out in ten minutes, then just drive off… Meet me at Macdonald's in the city centre at nine o'clock, if there's a problem, I'll call you on this phone." She picks up a small mobile phone which she drops back onto the passenger seat.

You watch her stuff the remaining parcels under her waistband and you notice her protruding ribs as she lifts her t-shirt up to strap two across her chest with masking tape.

Your palms are sweaty so you grip the steering wheel more tightly and make a u-turn . Your eye is fixed on the building in the side mirror. A few passers-by peer into the car and try to get a good look at you. You lock the doors.

Ten minutes pass and you wonder how much longer you should wait.

A few minutes later you clock two community coppers heading your way, so you mess with your phone. The only person you can think of calling is Mel. The phone rings and, whilst you wait for her to answer, you sweat some more.

Fuckin' pick up.

"Are you all right, sir?" One of them pokes his head in the small gap in the window on the passenger side.

You point to the phone and mouth that you're taking a call.

"You can't park here, sir. Move along please."

You nod and mouth 'just getting directions.' He moves back onto the pavement and waits there for you to finish. You give up trying to reach Mel and start the engine. The last thing you need is for Alex to come out with this jobsworth supervising.

You hear a car backfire — or was it a gunshot?

You drive slowly round the block and as you get to the backend of the house where you'd dropped Alex off, a small figure in a blue hoodie scales the fence and starts running down the pavement. You speed up and overtake her. She sees you, grabs the door handle and dives into the back seat.

Shortly after, two lads come out onto the pavement. They look up and down the street. You're moving at a leisurely pace. When you're some distance away, Alex climbs over the seat into the front. Her t-shirt and hoodie get dislodged as she slides down. The butt of a gun, and stuffed white envelopes strapped to her back are visible. She sees the direction of your glance and pulls her clothing down.

"Lucky you came round when you did — thanks! One more drop."

"What happened there?" you ask, your head indicating the direction you've come from.

"Tried to jump me, didn't they? Had to shoot the fucker in the foot."

"You all right?" You're shocked but this is not the time to go into it.

She doesn't answer, points the way round to the next place.

"Park here," she says pulling her hoodie up. "This is a double."

"What do you mean?"

"Like I said, a double." She reads the confusion on your face and sighs, "I need you to come."

You remove the key from the ignition and follow her. She thrusts a rucksack into your hands and indicates for you to follow her. You don't look into the bag but focus on her small head. The golden curls mock you, her stride's strong and confident. For a moment you kid yourself that you're her protector. She knocks once on the door and tries the handle. The door creaks open into a surprisingly clean and tidy, stylish living room. The white and cream décor suggest order and makes you relax a little. A large man in his thirties occupies the middle of a cream leather sofa. He nods at you both and points to the table.

Alex nods towards the glass coffee table, you rest the rucksack on it. She frowns, so you open it. The man's eyes are glued to it, he rubs his large belly beneath the brown check shirt. You tip four brown packages onto the table. The man drags the table towards him.

"Danny!" he shouts, without moving his head towards Danny who seems to magically appear from the back of the room beside the window. His brown leather jacket blending him in with the brown and cream velvet curtains. He's a tall slim lad, not more than nineteen. He swaggers forward with a small bag, it looks heavy. Alex counts the money inside and checks three guns packed into the side pockets.

"You staying for a poke, sweetheart?"

You step forward to remind him that she's just a child, she warns you off with a look, so you imitate her as she backs out.

"Some bodyguard!" they snigger as you leave.

"Run!"

"What?" You've already picked up speed and aim the remote at the car and she slides in before you have your door open. It's not immediately evident why you're running. She again directs you to another street and a few turns into a different area.

"Ditch the car."

She disappears across the street and eventually becomes a blue blob in a market street. You dither for a moment, but the sight of a long lanky lad heading towards you gets your brain juices flowing. You look for the signs to the bus station. The unspent fuel money is more than enough to buy a coach fare to Victoria.

You doze on and off all the way to London and, during your waking moments, try to make sense of the past twelve hours. Maybe after you get paid, you'll tell Andy that it's not for you. It's not as though you know anything — I mean, you don't even know where you went to.

Andy will understand.

BETTY
30 JULY

I open my eyes, I'm too scared to move.

The warmth will turn to cold wee the minute I get out. Makes me shiver just thinking about it.

I don't want to find Angela didn't really come yesterday. She was here all of one hour with the grandkids. Imagine, one hour after all this time.

Angela's a good girl, she takes good care of my financials. But I have to say, she's a lousy mother. Them bleeding brats all over the place. I had a good mind to clip their ears. The older one didn't come. I expect she's got better things to do. If she's anything like her mother, she needs to go on the pill. Better safe than sorry, I'd say.

Maybe I could spend the day in bed. Them pads they brought are right handy in the night. I suppose it's all right if I just let it flow like — only number ones mind. I can't imagine keeping a parcel of poo all day in the pads.

Angela was a right slapper. I know I shouldn't say bad things about my own daughter. But truth is, all the lads from miles around came sniffing round her. Bleeding slut. Raised her better than that.

At least she came to see me. She's a good girl is Angela.

The carer might come again today. Supposed to come twice a day to help me with meals and that. Get the sheets off the bed. It's like having a maid. Except she's not at my beck and call.

Wonder if the nurse will drop in. I heard the carer yesterday on the phone to the office. Telling them the nurse hasn't been for three weeks. That Schola never came back. She needs to scholar herself not to tell bleeding lies.

Maybe the carer will bring me breakfast in bed. That'd be nice.

My Harry. Now, he was a good egg. On Sunday morning, he'd bring me breakfast in bed. Mind you, he was only good for peeling potatoes and boiling eggs. Still — it's the thought that counts, and he was good for a tumble every afternoon.

The carer that came yesterday was fast. Gave me a lick and a promise by the bathroom basin. When she finished, I told her I'd finish off myself. She was hoppin' mad. But of course. They teach them to be nice to old people, so she couldn't really say what she thought.

Ohh! Must have dropped off to sleep again. What time is it? Oh, bloody hell! She's been and left me a cold cup of tea. Maybe I should get up.

The sun's already gone too high for me to enjoy through my bedroom window. As I go through my morning rituals, I try not to notice the puddle in the bed.

Bleeding girl should have woken me up. Now where's my puffer?

She's left porridge in the pot — looks like cement. Can't even warm it up. I'll eat the cheese sandwich she left for lunch. Make my own cup of tea. I'm not in the mood for Lorraine today. I don't want cheering up, thank you very much.

The bin is overflowing with dirty pads. Do I call the office to ask about the carer? I'll eat my sandwich and then see.

Don't know what's wrong with me today. I've slept the day away. No bleeding carer. Maybe I'll have to sleep in the recliner chair. I can't get those sheets off — they're wet through.

Where's that bleeding Angela when I need her? It was mum's idea to call her Angela. She looked like a little angel, she said. I should have called her something like...

I'll try her number. I'm sure she'll be round in a few minutes.

"Hello, hello — bleeding answer machine."

I'll call the agency.

"It's Betty Lyons, yes, that's me. No one's been today. I need help..."

Bleeding woman tells me that they are very short staffed and have to prioritise. Does she think I'm bleeding paperwork?

"Now that I've agreed to have your help, you're letting me down badly."

Maybe I should try some tears.

It works, someone's coming 'round to change my sheets. Well, at least that's today taken care of.

These days the time just seems to slip away from me. The carer said it's Thursday but last time I spoke to someone, I can swear they said Monday. I wonder if this is what happens when your time is up.

Maybe everyone else knows I'm checking out soon, but no one wants to tell me. All that pc business, they need to tell the bleeding truth.

Angela was here Sunday to collect all my cards and that. I was so happy to see her I didn't ask enough questions. She said she'll take care of things.

Carer said she won't be back today.

What did she leave for supper? Another bleeding sandwich. Now where's Harry's bottle of whisky? Might as well have a drink.

Oh! That's done it — can't open the bleeding bottle. Arthritic, good-for-nothing fingers.

I know, I'll stand by the door and get someone passing.

I open the door a crack just in time to catch that coloured one. The big one with the loud voice. At least I can understand what she says.

"Hello — you couldn't help me a minute with my bottle?"

"What bottle is that, Betty? Ah! Jim Beam ah ah whisky? Are you supposed to be drinking that?"

"I can bleeding well drink what I want."

"So why don't you open the bleeding bottle yourself then?"

Oh dear, that's gone and done it. I expect she won't be opening it.

"What's the bloody use? I just sit here day and night waiting. Bloody waiting. Might as well have a drink."

I don't mean to, but I start crying. If I knew tears could be this effective, I would have started years ago.

She helps me into the bathroom and gives me a right proper wash and helps me on with my nightie. When I tell her about my bed, she strips it, puts the lot in the washing machine. She tries to dab the mattress with a wet soapy sponge but I know it won't do much. Then she gets the dryer out and dries it all up and puts clean sheets on.

If I'd known she was this efficient, I would have been nice to her ages ago.

She is bossy though.

"What are you having for supper then, Betty?"

Before I can answer, she's got the freezer open. Thankfully, Angela did the monthly shop on Sunday before she disappeared with my cards. Whilst the steak is defrosting, she peels and cuts potatoes and makes homemade chips. She clears the table and makes me sit at the table.

I don't dare refuse.

"So, what's your name?"

"Beauty."

Honestly, I don't know where they get these names from. She's very nice. But I wouldn't call her beautiful.

Not with that large nose, eyes, everything really. But she's neat and tidy. I can say that much.

She stares back at me. I suppose she's sizing me up too. She does have a bit of an attitude. That much has to be said about her.

"Eat up, then I'll do your dishes and tuck you in with your whisky. Okay?"

Perfect plan. But what if she robs me blind?

"Thank you."

"What happened to your carers today?"

"They only came this morning."

I hate to be pitied. Especially by strangers. So, I look at something else.

When she's tucked me in and hung up the sheets and that, she says she'll be back in the morning to check on me on her way to her client.

"There's nothing here you know — don't keep money in the house."

I didn't mean to blurt it out like that. Fortunately, she misses my meaning. I watch her rolling buttocks find their way to the door and out into the corridor. Then I dream of Harry laughing and carrying on. I expect he's got some floozie up there. When I wake up, I'm hopping mad — it's all right for some.

At about ten the next morning, Beauty comes back and finds me sitting on the edge of the bed trying to get out of my nightie. We go through yesterday's rituals.

"How comes you're not at work?"

"I've been suspended from work."

"What for?" I expect she's been caught stealing or something. Can't trust these coloured ones.

She doesn't answer. She just rubs the flannel on my back harder than necessary. She's not rough or nothing like that, just heavy-handed. Expect she's used to that — needs it to get herself washed and that — she's so... large.

She puts the clean sheets on the bed and bungs the wet ones in the machine. She makes me brunch, 'cause it's eleven-thirty by the time we finish everything. Sausage, fried tomatoes — don't know what she did with the baked beans — they're right tasty, potato, a fried egg. I gobble up the lot.

"I can't afford to pay you, you know."

She rings Angela from her mobile. They talk for a bit and then she hangs up and Angela rings.

Angela asks if I know a Beauty-somebody-or-other. I say yes and how helpful she's been. She wants to know would I like Beauty to continue to look after me. I hesitate for a moment. Should I tell her she's been suspended from work?

I say yes.

When Beauty comes later, I sit her down. I let her know she needs to come clean or I'll ring the agency.

"You know Abi?" I blink trying to think why I should know her. "You know, the one who lives there." She points so I know right away who she means — that other one. "She lied about me at work and said that I'd hurt someone. I don't know why the resident thinks it was me, but I didn't look after her that whole week. She probably got mixed up

— you know how it is with old… " she checks herself. If she'd said it, I'd have shown her the door.

"Why should I believe you?"

"Well you don't have to — it's up to you. The agency has no carers - so you can just wait until they do."

She gets up to leave. I feel sorry for her. Or is it me really that I feel sorry for?

"Maybe we could give it a trial? One week, mind!"

"See you at six-thirty then." And with a flash of skirt, she's gone.

LUKE
JUNE

It's still light outside when you arrive back in London and you fancy a beer and something to eat, but you dare not use Andy's money and yours is tucked away for vital stuff for Charlotte.

You ring Andy when you're home to tell him you're back. While you wait, you stand under the shower for ages, willing the hot water to dissolve your memory. He comes around within an hour, and you're both in stone-washed jeans and white T-shirts.

"Alex just phoned. She got back all right. Said you did well," Andy sniffs.

You feel a warm sensation in the pit of your stomach as you imagine the five hundred in your hand. You can't remember when last you saw that amount of money. You visualise it stashed up in notes held together in rubber bands, a hundred in each, crisp ten-pound notes.

"She told me you had to ditch the car. That was the right thing to do. Can't trust those fuckers up north. Know what I mean?"

You put the keys on the table.

"What the fuck's that?"

"Car keys."

"I know they're car keys, shithead. What did you fuckin' bring them for?"

You shrug.

"You were supposed to leave them in the vehicle. How's the dealer going to move it now? Well that's coming out of your wages — one-fifty for a new set of keys."

You watch the veins in his neck twitching as he counts out the money.

"Two-fifty, that's it."

"You said five hundred."

He sits down beside you and cups the back of your head in his hand.

"Listen, my son, you didn't do nothing on your own. You had to be told where to go and that. You even brought back the car keys. Next time — okay?"

"That's the thing — see, there isn't going to be a next time. It's not for me. I can't be dealing with guns and drugs. It's not my scene."

His veins twitch again, and he clenches his jaw.

"You don't get it — I mean, you're owing us money."

"I owe you fuck-all."

"First, I get you wheels to do your job, not to mention the petrol money and then you cost me because you bring the fuckin' keys back... "

"Who's us?"

"The guys are gonna love you. Shit for brains — I can't even tell them you want out or — shit, I don't even dare mention it. Just stay and work off the money you owe. Okay?"

He cups the back of your head again. You don't answer but reach for your tobacco, you spill a pinch on your clothes and some lands on Andy's jeans. He removes his hand from your head and brushes it off in disgust. You manage to get the tobacco rolled up, less tighter than usual and concentrate on lighting it.

"By the way, we ran out of space, so I've stashed some stuff in here. You should see the look on your face — ha ha! Fuckin' priceless. Next job's in a few days. In the meantime, if you want to earn yourself some more dosh — refer anyone needing a fridge, stove and that sort of thing. It'll earn you thirty. Especially if they live here — it's near for Brian to cart it over like."

He looks at the money on the table, and you grab it before he can find something else to charge you with. After he's gone, you spend a long time with your head in your hands.

The next day you open an account for Charlotte at the Nationwide and pay in two hundred pounds. You mail the account details and a greeting card to mum and send her twenty pounds in cash, folded neatly inside the card.

Here's half the money I owe you, I'll send the rest next week

Just look after the details for me, Mum.

Love Luke

She calls you just as you're preparing for your next trip, this time to Liverpool.

"Lukey, you didn't have to pay it back. I have enough. Ah, isn't that nice what you did for Charlotte? I promise I'll go and see her before she goes back to school. That's something I wish I'd done for you, your own bank account — you working now?"

"Kinda, you all right, Mum?"

"You sure you're all right? You don't sound it."

"I'm fine, Mum."

She blows kisses down the phone, ends the call.

Liverpool is much the same as Manchester, except this time you go down on the train and pick up a car when you get there. This one's a BMW one series — it's not that old but has gone on some long journeys with not-so-careful drivers. You're surprised at how glad you feel to see Alex.

"All right?" She nods back at you and directs you for the next six hours. This time the customers come out to meet the car and the exchanges take place in the street except for the last house.

It's a big house, you imagine four bedrooms. You park the car at a car dealer's at the end of the day and remember to leave the key beneath the driver's mat. You travel back to London separately.

Again, Andy drops in to pay you. This time it's four hundred.

"Why's it short?"

"You're asking me, why it's short? What do you fuckin' well think? The money was short this time — Alex was meant to bring back twenty grand — what do I get? Fuckin' nineteen-eight hundred."

"That's not my fault — I don't handle the money."

"But you was there — with her. You owe a hundred each."

You wonder who can get you out of this. There's always going to be something. Plus, if you get caught with anything — he'll just land you in it. After all, some of the stuff's somewhere in your flat, but try as you may, you can't find it.

The next day you pay in another two hundred pounds into Charlotte's account, send the other twenty to mum and ask her to pop into the NatEast so you can make her a signatory on Charlotte's account. You put the rest on a master prepaid card which you register in your cousin's name — Mathew, you apply for a passport in his name with your pic and then you get all the documents on-line. You register a post box in Mathew's name to receive all the new documents.

BEAUTY
2 JULY

That Thursday morning, I had been dreading going to work because I'd have to deal with that Abi. When I got there for my twelve-hour shift, I spent a long time in my locker pretending to sort out my bag, comb what-what when that one walked in. She pretended she couldn't see me and went straight to her locker. Me, I know she saw me because, like I always say, I am a big girl. I slammed the locker shut. Still she ignored me. I went to stand behind her.

"'Morning, Abi." When Abi did not answer, I tapped her on the shoulder. "I said, good morning, Abi."

"Oh, sorry — I was far away… " I tried to be professional.

"We at work now — it's better if we act like nothing's wrong. If Nurse Katie finds out… "

"Ah! Do I care? Maybe you can tell Oprah!"

I was surprised that she knew about Oprah — after all, she says that she never watches television.

"That's a stupid thing to say — I need to work — maybe you don't."

She left after that and I'm sure she went to look for Nurse Katie. Me, I wasn't bothered. Let her try me and see what happens.

LUKE
16 JULY

You are sitting outside, enjoying what you think are the last weeks of the summer sun. Cecilia stops by for a short chat. She's excited because Pablo's coming home soon.

"He'll be back in time for the baby."

"That's nice," you say.

She stops with you for a bit while she's waiting to meet a friend. They're going to shop for baby clothes.

A large, black woman steps out of Babel into the sunshine and stops to chat with Cecilia.

"Is Pabi not back yet?" The woman asks Cecilia.

"He'll be here in time for the baby."

"That's gonna be a big baby, you look like you're ready to drop!"

"Just going out for the last shop for the baby," Cecilia responds, standing up to leave.

"Me, I need a new stove," the big one says. "I've got to get it today. Okafor tried but he can't fix the old one — he likes me to cook his food."

You jump up.

"You're looking for a stove? If you buy a new fridge as well, I can get you a discount — can talk to the owner."

"Is it new or what?"

"New stuff. Did you want to get it today?"

"I mean I can come today and see the things."

You lead the way and she matches you step for step into the shop. You tell her to wait at the entrance and you work your way to the back where Brian is outside having a drink. He nods at you and scratches himself before he removes his hand and picks up his can again.

"I can give her a discount — you sure she lives round yours?"

"I'll be wanting my thirty-pound referral fee."

"Yeah, yeah, no sweat — the bigger the discount, the less you'll get."

The woman buys a secondhand fridge and a stove for cash. She counts out the money and hands it over.

"Thanks, man — tell you what, since she's handed over cash, I'll give a hundred for both. How's that?"

The woman is hovering nearby, and you wonder if it matters that she might have overheard your conversation. You take the hundred and pay it onto your card.

You're doing at least three trips a week now and the money's adding up. You never get the five hundred per trip that Andy had originally promised, but at least you're taking in nine hundred to a grand a week. That, plus your back-dated benefits money, means your card is loaded with three and a half grand. Charlotte's account has six hundred in it.

This coming week you plan to top up Charlotte's account with another two hundred and you need to get some things sorted. You offer to do an extra trip. So, instead of coming home from Liverpool, you head out to Hull where you work with Ryan. He's not much older than Alex and he likes to talk — he sounds like he samples the merchandise.

When you get back, Andy has news.

"You're going to do trips on your own now — means more money — a grand each trip."

More like seven hundred

"What about Alex?"

"What about Alex? Fuckin' search me — what do you know?"

"I only see her on trips. That's why I'm asking you, innit?"

"If you hear from her, let me know. She owes us a fuckin' load."

You think Andy knows more about Alex. She might even be dead or sold on to another gang. You've heard they do this sometimes. You feel sorry for her, but you have your own problems.

You don't come home anymore, preferring to check into the local Travelodge in your work areas instead. Forty quid is not too much for a good night's kip and another twenty for a Harvester roast and a pint. You've even bought yourself some new kit. But you keep it tucked into your rucksack.

You're in a different city each night. You like Liverpool and Hull best because the clients pay by bank transfer so you can't be short-changed. When you get to Wolverhampton, you text mum to meet you.

"Mum, I'm going away soon — I have to." You stare straight ahead so that you don't have to see her pain. She looks thin and yellowy from old bruises on her face and arms. Her dirty-blonde hair is dull and hangs, looks like it needs a wash. She doesn't look anything like the mum who used to pick you up from school. You watch her hands shake as she lights a fag, not daring to look into her eyes.

"Oh, Lukey, you've got yourself in trouble, haven't you?"

"Just listen for a minute will you, Mum — I can't tell you where I'm going but as soon as I'm settled, I'll send for you. You've got to get away from that man — and all this. And maybe I can get Charlotte — don't know yet."

"Oh, Lukey..."

"Mum, when the time comes, I'll send you my bank card where they pay the social security and that. I want you to draw the money every time it gets paid in — all of it, Mum. Then you pay in the cash — cash only, Mum, into an account that I'll give you. Are you listening, Mum?"

"What account is that then, Lukey?"

"I'll give you the details later." You're yet to set up a new account that won't be linked to your name.

"Promise I'll see you again?"

"I'll send for you, Mum."

"I don't want to be a burden... "

"Mum, please... I love you, Mum. I gotta go. Do you need some money?"

You slip three hundred into her bag.

"Get-away money, Mum. You can't go to my flat, no matter what, Mum. If they find you there, I don't know… "

Before she can ask you for details. you kiss her cheek and hug her tightly then walk away, you feel her eyes on your back. You've learnt the art of vanishing into empty streets.

Before seven that evening, you're delivering in Manchester. You now keep a gun beneath your seat. You still don't know the first thing about using it, but it somehow reassures. You keep things sweet with the customers and small dealers, make sure they send the money, then leave. The next few evenings you carry out drops in Leeds, Liverpool and Hull. By Sunday morning, you're back at your gaff.

Andy tries to pay you by account, so you lie and tell him you're waiting for your new driver's license so's you can open a new bank account. You have to keep as much money as cash. Besides, the other one's linked to your benefits and you always worry that the benefits office will do a check and find all the extra dosh. You've also heard about the latest scams involving bank details — you wouldn't put anything past Andy.

When the licence arrives, it's in your dead cousin's name as planned and you open a Barkers and an FSBC current account and savings accounts Nationals and Northshire. Then you look into opening accounts online. You open two more then spread the money around each of

186

the accounts. Each week you buy Euro from each of the different post offices in all the places that you visit. You decide that five hundred is an amount that someone like you can change without raising eyebrows. Some of the counter staff try to engage you in chatter about where you might be going for your holiday. Your answer is always the same — Spain for a week. But you know that you'll be miles away from Spain. When the time comes.

PABLO
27 AUGUST

I stayed another week after mum was discharged. Alejandro promised to call me if anything changed. I booked the flight and took the coach to Malaga. Living like we did meant that we hardly checked the news and I arrived at the airport in the middle of a traffic controller strike. There was only one flight a day to London and mine had been bumped up to midnight — if I was lucky.

I spent a day and a night with the British tourists trying to get back to their lives in England. The television screens in the departure lounge were tuned to Sky News. I absently watched the images flashing on and off — the familiar advertisements reminded me of what I had missed. I thought of Cecilia and imagined how surprised and excited she'd be when I got in. I thought about her hair — I threw my jacket over my lap for the sake of the family sitting opposite me.

I started paying more attention to the news, hoping that it would control my thoughts. That's when I noticed the repeated reference to a fire. It was huge. I mean there were ten fire crews working on it, but the flames kept licking upwards. I listened to two guys beside me.

"That was deliberate, that was."

"You reckon?"

"Ten crews failing to control it — what do you think?"

"Maybe because of substandard materials or... "

I thought, that was an odd thing to say, so scrutinised the screen to see what the two guys were talking about. The room quietened down slowly — a few younger guys continued a conversation and loud laughter and in the back providing a macabra soundtrack to the video of a building with the windows on several floors breathing out orange flame. A middle-aged woman came to stand beside us to get a better view.

"Three people have died already. Poor sodding bastards!"

"Where is it?" the two guys had started chatting with the woman

"No idea."

One of the guys moved towards the television and turned the volume up. We were drawn forward, our eyes staring, whilst we waited through other news for the story about the fire. Then it started -

"Shh!" The middle-aged woman turned to the group at the back.

"Shortly before one a.m. on Wednesday morning,

A bonfire erupted in a tower block in West London."

The presenter paused and we heard the building crackling as it disintegrated. There were screams in the background. Sirens faded in and out. The more we saw, the more we wanted.

"At least twenty people have died, and the death toll is expected to rise."

The camera showed the front of the building then dropped to the front lawn.

"Wait! Wait!" It was someone else's voice. "Dios mio! It can't be — please rewind. Rewind."

"Calm down, mate. What is it — do you know that place?"

I nodded not able to speak.

"Somebody, get him some water — quick, quick."

I don't know if I fainted or just switched off. The whole of the front was on fire — that was our flat. My woman. My baby. When I recovered, I noticed that they had taken my passport out of my pocket and negotiated with the check-in desk for me to take the next flight out. I don't know if I thanked them enough, but they bumped me up to the front of the queue, so I was the first one on after the families with babies. Until the plane took off, I repeatedly tried Cecilia's number and left a thousand messages for her. Pleading, demanding she call me back, predicting that she would be okay. I gave up when the fasten seatbelts sign came on.

The last time I had prayed was when my mother had her stroke. I stared out the window.

"Hail Mary, full of grace... "

I shook my head at the hostess.

"The Lord is with thee.

Bedita tu eres entre todas las mujeres... "

I thought maybe God would hear me better in Spanish. The man next to me put on his headphones and watched the movie, looking at me occasionally as if he thought I was mad. The minutes fell like lead. At last, the captain announced the landing. The air hostess signalled to me and another man to sit in the seats near the exit.

At the airport, on the train, all I could see were pregnant women with long dark brown hair. I felt the stab as I watched their men fuss around them. Cecilia smiling, at the height of passion, angry and standing naked never left me all the way to West Park Station.

I ran the rest of the way.

BEAUTY
26 AUGUST

Early that morning, my phone pinged when I was dressing. I knew before I read it, it was a sweet message from Okafor.

Miss you, darling, sorry, I couldn't talk last night. See you soon, O.

He was always thinking of me, even when he was there with his people, there in Nigeria.

Missing you too, Okafor. Am here with Liam, twenty-four hours.

Then it was time to start work.

"'Morning, Liam. How are you today?"

"Let me sleep."

"Yesterday, you said, let me sleep. You didn't eat. You didn't wash. Today you must wash, and I'll make for you scrambled eggs."

"The thought of eggs makes me want to throw. Go away woman! Let me die."

"Die? You want to die?" Liam was making me cross. "I'm going to call your GP."

"Good luck, they never come. Just promises — let me sleep."

"Then I'll also call your sister, I can see her number here on your cellular."

He didn't answer, this Liam. He just covered his head with the duvet. It must be bad to be old — duvet, when it's so hot. And no washing — two days now. I called the GP, they wanted to tell me they're busy what-what. I told them if they don't send a doctor, I'll go there and get one. They said the doctor will be here at two this afternoon.

Better.

I found a bowl and warm water and went to wash Liam. I thought he was going to say 'leave me, bossy woman' but he just lay there. I made him sit in the chair then stripped the bed. I think he was just wanting to die — no coughing, no diarrhoea — eee! Just poorly. It's bad to get old.

The woman doctor came. Dr Martins. I saw her looking, looking around the house. She wanted to make faces — but the house was clean. I know. I cleaned it myself. She looked at me as if she thought I can't talk.

"Ah, you're here to see Liam. He's here." I took her upstairs to Liam's room. "He's not eating, he's just lying in bed. Normally by this time, he's washed and dressed when I get here. And he'll be telling me, Beauty, do this, Beauty what-what, but look at him."

I opened the door and let the doctor go in. Liam was there, the covers over his head. Pretending to be asleep.

"Liam, the doctor is here." No answer, so I pulled the covers. He was holding tight his side, me, I was pulling.

The doctor was waiting with a smile that was getting tired. Then he let go — two days, no food can make you weak.

The doctor sat and I stood by the door. She kept looking at me, maybe she wanted me to go, but me, I knew the answers and Liam was not talking. She took her stethoscope checked him, temperature and blood pressure. Then she smiled at me as if we have secrets, me and her.

"Everything is okay, has he lost weight?"

"Well, it's only two days — can a person lose weight in two days?" I thought that might be useful information, because me, I was getting too big.

"Well, not exactly. But we need to make sure that he gets enough nutrition. I'll prescribe some drinks that he can have. Are you here all the time?"

"Ah no, I only slept here last night because I could see Liam, he's sick. If I need to sleep here again then I need to be paid. I can't sleep here for nothing. I also have another client, I only saw her for thirty minutes yesterday. Somebody needs to arrange... "

"So, did you talk to the agency about this?"

"What agency? Me and Liam we just arranged."

"In that case, I'll try and get a social worker out to see him and have a chat with you."

"Better, it's getting too much. Me, also I need to have time to do my things."

"Could you stay one more day?" I nodded, because, I was also worried about Liam. "I'll give you a prescription, if you don't mind going to the pharmacy. I'm sure that you can leave Liam for an hour or so."

I was happy to help but I wasn't sure how this was going to go on. Whilst I was out, I got some clean clothes and my books. I was starting Access to Nursing in September, so I was already reading books that could help. It would be a big embarrassment if I failed before I even started the nursing.

Okafor was telling me, "No need, I can look after you, what-what." I know these men — they can change like the British weather. If he became like the winter here, what would I do? His people could even say that he needs a Nigerian woman. We had been living together for some months and still, he was not saying we are getting married. No, I couldn't just sit. I have to work hard so that maybe end of next year, I can bring my children. Even if we got married, he could even say, "Those are not my children, I can't look after them, phone their dad." These men can surprise you anytime.

I walked to the pharmacy with the prescription and while I was waiting, I did shopping for Liam. Then I went to the flat to collect my things. I thought that I had left the windows shut, but the bedroom window was wide like a hungry bird. And the bed looked like someone was there the night before. That is not how I made the bed. Ah ah, what now? I checked the bathroom it was the same.

I locked the door and left. Maybe I had made the bed, funny like that because I was missing Okafor.

I decided it was a good time to check on Betty. I took the key from the key safe and went in. The smell of wee greeted me. I left my bag by the door. Betty was sitting on her bed. She looked like she had been swimming in her nightdress.

"Hello, Betty, what is happening?"

"Oh, Beauty, I'm so glad you came. I was just thinking I need to change my clothes today. You wouldn't get me my blue cardigan from the drawer, would you? The pink one's disappeared."

"Betty, you forgot that I washed it yesterday? Anyway, you need a shower. Come!"

"You can just let me wash at the basin, like I normally do."

"Not today. You're having a shower."

"You don't come in here telling me what I can do and what I bleeding well can't"

"Uh uh, Betty, today I have no time to argue. We need to do chop-chop."

"Chop, chop? What am I? Bleeding sack of potatoes?"

"Come, Betty."

I got clean clothes and we went to the bathroom whilst she was calling me names. Coloured this, stupid that. But I am not the one who needs help. So, I kept quiet. When she was in the hot water, she also kept quiet. She didn't look at me while I helped her to get dressed and dried her hair. I pulled her chair by the window in the sun.

"I can't see the television from here."

"You need some sunshine. You can have your breakfast there."

"You're very cruel — punishing me for wetting the bed."

"You can sit there for a while. After an hour, you can sit in your chair."

Lucky, I had put plastic on the mattress otherwise... I was glad I was going to be a nurse, this caring job is hard work. And clients like Betty, they're never grateful. Anyway, if this was my granny, I would want someone to help her. Lucky also, I had arranged with the daughter and she was paying me. A bit less than usual, but it was better, because me, I can't work for free. Lucky that Betty told her daughter said she wanted me to come, because of that problem at the nursing home, I couldn't get a reference.

I think Abi had something to do with it. Maybe she lied, I don't know. But they wrote me a letter and said they are still investigating. I don't know what they are investigating because they haven't asked me anything. Okafor said I shouldn't worry, he can look after me and my whole village back home. Me, I don't want to wait for him to give me money. I will have to go to him and say Okafor, please, this, Okafor, please, money for that. Then he will decide how much I need to buy things for my kids and even my pant and makeup.

No, thank you!

So, I had two clients of my own. Maybe when Liam was better, I'd find two more clients because the money is not enough. The agency said I can't work for them while the investigation is still pending. Nurse Katie called me last week and said she knew it wasn't me who did it because I was with another resident at that time. Maybe she also thought it was Abi, but she didn't say anything.

Ah yah, some people!

She asked me if I have any evidence. Of course, I don't have evidence. She is the one that did the allocation that day, and how would I find evidence in my flat?

I saw Abi in the corridor on Monday, she pretended she didn't see me, then she ran to her flat and she was trying to open the door quickly before I passed her, but she dropped the key. Me, I laughed, shame! If she didn't do anything, she wouldn't be running away from me like that. She is scared that I will ask her. That is evidence, but I don't think that will help Nurse Katie.

I helped Betty back to her chair and turned on the television. I made her some food and left.

I crossed the road to Liam's house and made him come downstairs and sit in the backyard. Me, I believe that sunshine is good for everything. Maybe when his brain is warmed with the sun, he will stop this 'I want to die' business.

He ate a little this, and a little that, and he drank some of the drink the doctor prescribed. It was time to call his sister. Someone from the family had to come. The phone didn't even ring.

"Liam, have you got another number for your sister?"

"I told you, she died last month."

"What of her children? Didn't you say you have another one?"

"She didn't have any children. I have no living relatives."

"Ah, ah, Liam, there must be someone."

"I tell you, there's not a living soul."

Now that was tough, if Liam died, who was I going to call? I wondered whether I should ask him, especially since he is talking about dying.

"If you're wondering what will happen if I die, I've left a will."

"So, you must give me the name of the lawyer — so I know who to call."

When he gave me the number, I called and told them that Liam is ill and that he's talking about dying. They tried to tell me that even if someone is talking about dying, it doesn't mean that they will die. But, I know when my grandmother talked about dying she died a few days later. I told him I want to be prepared. The lawyer came on the phone and said he would come to see Liam on his way home. He had been meaning to stop by to see Liam as their fathers used to be friends.

Better.

I let the lawyer in at about seven and they talked with Liam. When he came out, he looked at me.

"So, you are Beauty? Liam speaks very highly of you. He said you saved him."

"Well, we are helping each other. Me, I need a job, he needs help, so I can also speak highly of him too. I am worried if anything happens to him — I will call you?"

"You do that."

The lawyer smiled and left. Liam was better after that, he ate his supper. And there was no fighting at bedtime. I went to Betty, gave her food and settled her.

I decided I'd spend one more night at Liam's. I went to my room and sat down to read, but the words in the book didn't change. The same sentence kept coming back and I didn't understand it. I gave up and prepared for bed. It was early, so I was lying there thinking about my children, my sister, Okafor, Betty, Liam, that silly Abi, money, round and round — it was like they were walking in a circle round my head until I fell asleep.

LUKE
26 AUGUST

You've a few days off. Mel's changed from psycho-bitch to semi-normal these days as you've been dropping the odd fifty quid into her account.

"I'll just stop by for a bit. Maybe we can go to MacT's and that?"

"Make sure you come by two, okay?" Mel answers.

Controlling fuckin' freak.

Mel and Charlotte are waiting for you outside Mac T's. Charlotte comes running towards you as soon as she spots you. You lift her up and swing her around.

"Daddy's special merry-go-round." You feel Mel's eyes taking in your new trainers and jeans from Primark. You've been careful not to be too flashy, you don't want Mel asking questions.

"Where did you say you were working again?"

"I didn't. I'm just doing odd jobs like delivery and that." You hope that she won't keep badgering.

"What time you coming back?" Mel asks. "I'll come and pick up Charlotte in about an hour. Make sure you wait outside with her."

"Come around four."

Mel looks as though she's going to argue, but that fifty you gave her last week is keeping her sweet. She nods instead.

"'Bye Charlotte!"

You and Charlotte go into Mac T's. It takes you about five minutes to order and another fifteen to eat your food. Then you take her to Selythe's Toyshop and buy her a dancing light-up doll and some clothes for the doll. Then you walk across the park and push Charlotte on the swings. Something that you've always wanted to do. You persuade her off with a promise of ice-cream and get back in time to find Mel parking her car in the MacT's car park.

If Charlotte feels suffocated by your extra hard, long hug, she doesn't show it. She hugs you back after you plant kisses on her cheeks and forehead.

"'Bye, 'bye, Daddy. Big hugs." She giggles and waves.

"'Bye, 'bye, Charlotte, kisses."

"Kiss, kiss Daddy." Her little voice haunts you all the way to the bus stop.

You collect your documents and rucksack from the left luggage at Victoria station and buy a ticket to Edinburgh. A quick stop in the toilet allows you to check your funds. You think about all the risks that you had taken and reassure yourself that you deserve it — all that pay that Andy had short-changed you.

You came up with the idea a month ago when you started doing solo trips. The thought reminds you of Alex and you briefly wonder what could have happened to her.

That first day you had twenty bricks of tightly-packed cocaine to deliver — twenty-five grand a brick. The checks on whether you'd delivered the right amount for the right payment were so tight that you had thought you wouldn't be able to pull it off. You worked out that one brick weighed a kilo, but each customer wanted to test the brick before you left it. You got a spoon to dig out the merchandise and always made sure that you left a little on the spoon which you replaced in a plastic bag in your pocket. Once you got in the car, you removed the remainder of the grains from the spoon. At the end of each day, you had about twenty to thirty grams which you sold for five to seven hundred-and-fifty pounds. Working five or six days a week, you earned about three grand tax-free. When you moved on to Liverpool, you offered to service the small towns on the way, your income rose to as much as five grand a night. You had made a total of a couple of hundred thousand in hard cash stashed in different accounts and bags at various airports and train stations. You'd have to keep coming back until you'd collected the lot. Maybe start a business when you get to your final destination.

When you get to Edinburgh, you take a taxi to the airport, where you buy a ticket from the British Airways sales desk. You purchase a one-way ticket to Malta. As soon as you're cleared through immigration, you check your phone.

Where are you? Call me. Mum.

You dial her number from one of your burner phones.

"Mum… "

"Oh, Lukey, where are you? Someone came round for you today. Graham's getting twitchy. Oh! Darlin,' it's all gone pear-shaped. Graham's talkin' about five grand."

"Slow down, Mum. Who did you see? What'd he look like?" You realise what a mistake it was for you to visit your mum. It was inevitable that Andy and his people would have someone to follow you and get to know your nearest and dearest. You remember it being referred to as an insurance policy.

"I don't know — I can't… But Graham said he'll shop you for five grand."

"Okay, Mum, Mum, just calm down okay. You can't phone me anymore okay. Just listen a minute. I'll phone you. Have you still got the money I gave you? Good, that's good — hello… "

You try to listen to the voice in the background, it sounds like more than one person. If they found your mum, it's just a matter of time before they get to Charlotte and Mel. You decide to call Mel from your normal phone before you destroy it You can just imagine all the questions she'd ask if you phoned her from another number. Besides, she doesn't know when to shut up.

"She's on a playdate with her friend from school. They were supposed to be back by now — I expect they're stuck in traffic — you know… everything all right? You've only just seen her — wait a minute, it's to do with all that money. I thought you seemed a bit flash — what have you gotten us into? Bloody hell — if you've… "

"Just shut up for a minute, will you? I can't bleeding well think. Call Charlotte's friend's mum and find out what's going on. I'll call you back in five minutes."

You snap at the bartender when he comes to take your order. What will you do? Mel rings you back.

"I said I'd ring you. Can't you listen for once? Where is she?"

"They just walked in after I put the phone down."

"Right, no more playdates. You stay in the house, both of you until I tell you what to do."

"I can't bloody well stay in the house, I've got to go to work… "

"Call in sick, say Charlotte's not well — whatever. Nobody in or out the house."

"You can't bloody well tell me what to do, I swear if you've… "

"Shut-up — stupid cow. Do what I'm telling you till I've worked something out."

She starts blubbering, it takes you a few minutes to calm her down and you manage to end the call, giving you time to think. You consider going back to round up your women — yes, Mel included — she won't let you take Charlotte on her own, but it's too risky. Perhaps you could send for them, but that's a problem — Mel blabs too much and your mum's a nervous wreck. They'd leave a trail as wide as Loftus Road.

Fuckin' hell.

ABI
26 AUGUST

After Beauty got suspended, they brought new staff. Nurse Katie put them in charge of me, I didn't understand, wo. I had been there the longest, so I should have been the one in charge. Also, I was told I would not be allowed to work alone. So, I went to ask Nurse Katie.

"You will be working under Sara. She's very experienced and you can learn a lot from her."

"But I am also experienced. I have been working here the past four years. She is new here."

"That's the decision from management, Abi. When you have time, I would like to go over your statement."

"What statement? Oh. The one about Beauty — I thought that was finished by now."

"What made you think that it was finished?"

"It's been a month — I just thought… "

"This is really serious; safeguarding is involved. This in ongoing — I can't believe this is happening, in the ten years that I've worked here I've never had safeguarding involved. In fact — no, this whole thing is stressing me out. Come tomorrow — about eleven, then we can go over your statement. Between now and then I want you to try to remember any detail that might help the investigation."

"Okay, I'll see you tomorrow." The sweat on my lip was growing and my pants felt wet. I went to the toilet to check if my period was early — nothing.

The rest of the day, wo, I just kept thinking about what Nurse Katie said. But I told the truth in my statement. I didn't have to lie. I had made sure that Mrs Jones believed that Beauty did it.

That day I was glad I was working a half-day because the people at work were being funny, wo. These days when I went into the staff room everyone kept quiet. Even those carers that I got along with stopped being friendly. I just kept quiet. I needed to do something different, I wondered what I could do. I could no longer visit Beauty. In fact, I was scared of her. The other time when I was talking to her, just telling her facts — she beat me. I ended up in A and E with cuts and bruises. I wanted to go to the police but all the witnesses said that I started the fight. Everybody is against me, except Kudjoe. But I don't see him much these days, he says he is busy with work, but I wonder if he has found someone else or maybe his wife has come from Ghana. It will be very lonely without his visits a few times a week. Anyway, I will try and find out what it is, about the real problem.

When I invited Kudjoe to my flat, he said he might come later. I decided to think about my business. I was planning another trip to Nigeria so, I went to Finsbury Park to check for some dresses for my shop, but they hadn't arrived yet. I went to the hair shops at the top of the road and bought some hair-food and a new wig. I thought maybe I should start to do what the other girls do — Beauty is always wearing wigs and weaves and her man is always there. I always used to see him parking his car at the flat when he finished work. I think these men find women with weaves and makeup more sexy. I thought about these things on the bus home. After I got off the bus, I stopped at Afda for some drinks and walked back, then sat on the bench in the sun in the front of Babel and watched people passing. I wondered whether they were happy.

I smiled hello at Pablo's girlfriend. She was pregnant, but where was Pablo? These men are all the same — white, yellow, black, pink, brown — I suppose he's got someone fresh and he'll marry her and spoil her life.

She was being too friendly with that boy from the ground floor — ah, they are friends now. We will see what will happen next. These young people don't waste time. I was sure that he was planning to use her. We used to see him always standing outside the door, begging for change. What did he want with her? Someone's woman, hey!

Pablo must come back, wo, and look after his woman and the baby.

Eh, eh, Beauty keeps going in and out of that house. That was the second time that I had seen her. I think that is the client she had said that she wanted to share with me. I don't think that's a good arrangement, if anything goes wrong you have no one to fall back on.

If she is still working there, I will report her.

I watched her cross the road. She didn't see me. I couldn't tell what she was up to just by looking at her. I decided to watch her for a few days before I told Nurse Katie. And I was planning on telling the agency too.

An hour later, I was still sitting on the bench when I saw her carrying Tescott shopping into the house across the road. She was definitely up to something. That Beauty, she thought she was great.

I waited an hour to see if she would come out again. She did not. So, I went inside to make some Ogusi soup. The soup reminded me of Nigeria. I thought about Okorie's mother. I had not phoned her to find out if she was better. I went to buy a phone card from the newsagent across the road.

She had no WhatsApp. I had to call five times before someone answered.

"Eh, how are you?"

"Who calling, please?" It was the woman that looked after her.

"It's her daughter from England. Tell Mummie, Abi — Okorie's wife."

She went to give her the phone and I heard her explaining who I was. Mummie was going deaf, I was shouting wo. It didn't help, so the maid had to come back and talk for her. She had got the money, praise God. They did scan, and she had gallstones. It seems Okorie found the money for operation. She is better now. She wanted to know when I would be back to Nigeria. I talked to her for a bit and the maid told me the things that Mummie needed. Just as I finished, Kudjoe arrived.

It had been regular, this thing with Kudjoe. If his wife came from Ghana at the end of the month, it would be finished. I decided to let him sleep all night. When he started getting what he wanted, he had begun to talk less. Just food and sex — that was all he was interested in.

I missed Beauty, no one to talk to and discuss my problems — this Kudjoe didn't have interest in anything. One day when I click, clicked he got cross. Then he told me that it shows that I don't respect him. His head started sweating, he took a washrag and wiped it before it started running on his collar. I think he can get very angry, very fast.

But, if he became violent or aggressive, I would have chucked him out. This time I'm going nowhere. He must have heard me thinking about him. He must have gone home to shower, because he was smelling fresh, wo. He reminded me of Tiger deo advert. I used to know someone who used it everyday, wo. But that was a long time ago.

"Eh, Abi. Come and sit beside me." He patted the sofa, so I sat close to him. "I have something to tell you." I tried to read in his eyes if it was good or bad. "I will tell you tomorrow morning." He smiled when he said that, I hoped it was something good.

He had bought me a television because he said that my flat was like a funeral place and he always needed to be watching something. That night he was cheering his football team and drinking malt. He didn't even speak to me the whole time. I brought some red wine from the kitchen — it was strong and soon we were a bit drunk. I went to the bedroom to get ready for bed. About an hour later, he came, undressed and slipped between the sheets. We slept — soon after, his fat fingers were touching, touching. It was not the same that night. Everything had changed.

BEAUTY
26 AUGUST

You know when you are sleeping at a client, you can't dream like you're in your bed. I kept waking up to check him. Then I woke up because I could hear many voices outside. It was dark, Liam was snoring. I went downstairs to see what was the noise.

Before I got to the lounge, a bright, orange light burst through the window at the top of the front door, like the sun was shining. My heart started to beat so hard. I opened the door.

Everything just hit me bah! Just like that.

People in their nighties, shouting and crying. Smoke, glass breaking. Big flames licking Babel. The smell of burning was just too too bad. I mean, I've seen fire before and they didn't smell like that — rotting meat. Like death!

I ran upstairs to call the fire brigade.

What would become of Betty?

I found my phone on the table. There were some missed calls from Okafor. He had to wait as I had urgent calls to make. I gave the fire brigade the address. Then I went to check on Liam.

"What's that racket? Sounds like a baby elephant going up and down the stairs."

"There's a fire across the road. I have to go and check on my client — she's in there I have to get her out."

"A fire? You said a fire." I hadn't seen him move so quickly in a long time.

"I don't want you to go outside, okay?" I made him put on his dressing gown then sat him in the front room by the window. "Make sure you don't move so that you're ready in case the fire brigade wants to evacuate."

Liam nodded his head. I think he just wanted me to leave so that he could watch the fire — at least something exciting for him. I locked the door in case he decided to come out. Then I left the key in the door just in case. I went across the street.

I had to get to Betty.

I went into the block and remembered that, in the fire training, they had said we should always use the stairs. The staircase was like a marketplace — people shouting and running down the stairs like cows. I pushed up against them. When I got to the fourth floor, I got stuck. There were maybe twenty people coming down at the same time and me, I was pushing, but it was too much for me. I had to stop. I got pushed down to the third floor. I stood in the corner and waited then I went back upwards.

I looked down and saw the firemen coming into the building. They were telling people to leave quickly. They were so busy I didn't think I should worry them. I thought that some of them might be on our floor. Nobody would know that Betty was in her flat unable to move. I panicked, maybe I had given her too much whisky and she was too drunk to walk to the door.

It's only when I got to the fifth floor, that I realised that I hadn't thought about how I was going to get her out of the building. Especially if she started to be difficult.

As I went up, there were less people and the fresher air made it easier to breath. I could hear the firemen running up the stairs as I was struggling up the last steps at the top.

Hey! They were fit, man.

As I opened the door to the seventh floor, one of them was shouting at me to leave the building. I turned back to the stairs.

"I have come to collect my client. She can't come out by herself."

"Show me where she is, then you have to leave."

I tried to run to the door, but my legs were tired. So, I just walked and pointed. We got to the door same time — me and him. I took the key out and opened the door. Betty was sitting in her chair. She looked funny, maybe she was drunk, I don't know.

"Betty, Betty wake up!" I started to go into the flat but the fireman pulled me back.

"Wait there. Can she walk?"

"Yes, but very slowly, it will take her ten minutes to get to the door. if you can carry her out it would be better."

"Leave her to me, please leave the building."

A voice was speaking then from his walkie-talkie. He stood outside Betty's door and I heard him asking for help. I mean Betty wasn't as big as me, but he wasn't going to be able to carry her out by himself. I offered to carry her legs. I think he was getting cross because, me, I was still standing there trying to help.

He pointed at the stairs and I knew I had to leave, I was confident that he would look after Betty.

I looked over at Abi's door, I hadn't seen her leaving the building and she didn't work nights. I hesitated. She had been so wicked to me. Maybe I should leave her. I stood outside her door wondering what to do. She was evil, yes, but...

The fireman was looking at me, so I decided to knock. I banged hard.

"Abi, Abi!"

When there was no answer, I tried the door. I started banging again, I thought if she didn't know there was a fire, she might think I had come to fight her. I kept banging the door.

"Fire, Abi, Fire!"

At last, she came out. Her eyes were as red as a tomato. Had she been crying? That Abi, she's a liar. I hadn't realised that afro was a wig. She was always commenting about my wigs and weave. Now I know she's always wearing a wig.

Heh!

"Abi, we must leave now, the building is on fire."

I could see that she didn't believe me, so I pointed at the fireman. I saw her eyes grow big. She went back in and after some minutes, she returned with her handbag.

Some people!

I could see the smoke coming from under the door of my flat. I thought for a minute about my things. The fireman was now pushing us towards the stairs, so I had no chance.

"What about Betty?"

"I have to go downstairs to collect the slide then I can slide her down the stairs," the fireman said.

"I can get it for you…"

"Leave! Now, both of you."

Abi had already reached the stairs. I followed her.

"Thanks, Beauty."

She put her hand on top of my arm. I put my arm down and stretched my mouth and showed some teeth.

"You would have done the same thing for me."

We walked down the rest of the stairs without speaking. I went in front so that she could not walk next to me. We were not friends, I only checked on her because she is a human being. That is all.

At last we got to the bottom. I thought I'd wait until they got Betty out. Maybe I could ask Liam and she could sleep in the lounge until the council could find her another flat. I crossed the road so that I could see both the fire exits. I didn't know which one they would bring Betty from. I was irritated when Abi followed me and came over.

"Eh, Beauty, I meant to ask you."

"What, Abi?" I tried to be polite, but you know how it is.

"What of Okafor?"

"What do you mean?"

Before she could answer, there was a hum of people crying and screaming altogether like they were singing a church hymn. The fire had reached the tenth floor and glass had started to crack. The building melted from the inside in front of us. My heart started to pound, what if they hadn't got Betty out? What about the fireman? Did he have time to leave the building? If I had stayed, I would have been stuck also.

We stood there, me and Abi, our mouths open like hungry birds.

The last few people ran out of the building from the fire exits that were on the sides of the building. Everybody cheered. I think we were all crying by then.

"Beauty, did you call Okafor? Did he manage to get out? I was just wondering because I saw you trying to get Betty out. And then you woke me up. I didn't see him leave. Did you get me out first?"

I blinked at her. What was she talking about?

"He's in Nigeria."

"No, I saw him today, afternoon. He had his suitcases. He was looking very tired, as if he came from Nigeria, maybe he needed to rest.

"You're lying. Do you think this is funny?"

I don't know how, but I found my hands around her throat. That stupid woman could make me go mad.

"No, please, Beauty. I'm telling the truth, wo. Please release me."

I held onto her collar with one hand, then pulled out my phone and dialled his number. It was going to voicemail. I tried again. Then again. Nothing.

I remembered the open window, the bed. It was Okafor. Maybe he wanted to surprise me. If I had known that he had been in there, I wouldn't have wasted my time with this stupid woman. I dropped the phone then I shook her and shook her until I thought her eyes would fall out and roll across the road.

Someone came from behind me and pinned my arms.

"Stop, just calm down, you'll kill her." It was Okafor's soft voice — the one he used when we were making love. The way he said his 'a's' — it was him.

I swung round so quickly, the man lost his grip.

But that wasn't Okafor. It was a tall light-skinned man in a fireman's uniform. I walked away.

He was dead.

I sat on the wall outside Liam's house and stared and stared at Babel. The people crowded round and all the ambulances, fire brigade and police people were running around the place. Shouting orders. The blue and red lights flashing like night flowers, flowers for the dead.

I can't be sure, but I thought that was Abi with two suitcases walking down the road, away from the fire.

Whilst I was worrying about Okafor, I forgot about Betty. Not for long, but I abandoned her. I remembered her again because, while I was waiting to speak to the social worker, I heard her mention duty of care. Who should I report Betty's death to? I mean, I thought that she was dead, they hadn't told me anything but I had heard nothing of her.

It was a painful night — I didn't sleep when I got back to Liam. All the time I was doing his care I didn't think about what I was doing. I couldn't tell you what I made for his breakfast or even lunch. It's hard to lose someone. Especially someone special like Okafor. I wondered who I should call — I had no number for his relatives in Nigeria. I remembered that his friend worked for the Newham Council. I managed to get hold of him and asked him to contact Okafor's family.

I sat in my room at Liam's house looking out the window at the building. I remembered how the flames were already in my flat whilst the main fire was on the fourth floor. It was paining me here, right here. It was painful to breathe, to think, so I prayed.

I prayed that the pain would go away. I prayed that Okafor's spirit would go and dwell amongst his ancestors' spirits. I felt a little better after. I suppose these things take time.

That morning I was sitting in the office down the road from Liam's house waiting to put my name on the list for rehousing. The social worker was very busy. I noticed another woman, she smiled at me, so I went to speak to her. I told her about Betty, and she put her name on the register to see if she might turn up somewhere. Some elderly people had been put in a home nearby. Then I explained that I was staying with Liam and I didn't think I should be there so, whilst I wasn't an urgent case, I needed to get something soon. I left my details with her and went back to Liam's house.

Then later I was walking back from Tescott shopping when I saw two women with three suitcases get into a car nearby. I couldn't believe what I was seeing. I stopped in the middle of the pavement and someone knocked me with their shopping. I heard them swearing, but I was so surprised by what I saw, that I didn't even want to respond.

That was definitely Abi. But were those her suitcases? Or was she helping someone? Where did she get those things from? I recognised the other woman as the social worker I had spoken to before. I had been so anxious that I had forgotten to ask her name, or maybe she had told me, and I didn't hear her.

I went to see the woman straightaway. I couldn't let Abi get away with any more nonsense. We were all suffering after losing our things and yet here was Abi with two suitcases of stuff.

"Hello, I came to see you last week about rehousing and also about my client that is missing."

"I'll follow up for you — we are quite busy, you know."

Then she started talking through her nose, you know how these people get trying to sound professional. I decided to soften her.

"If it wasn't for your name, Mukai, I wouldn't have known that you were from home. Do you speak Shona?"

She kept quiet for a minute.

"Yes, I do."

We talked for a while about living in the UK and so on. Then I thought she was ready.

"I know you can't talk about clients, but the other day I thought I saw you with a friend of mine. Her name is Abi."

"You might have… "

"She must have been one of the lucky ones to get housing, and it seems that she must have had a big donation. I saw you giving her a lift the other day with lots of suitcases."

"How did you say that you knew Abi?"

I ended up telling her how I had saved her life but that she didn't care about anybody but herself or she could have saved my boyfriend's life. She looked very worried, and I know she wanted to ask me more information, but she might have been worried about this confidentiality thing that gets in the way of a good story.

I left her after that and promised to check after a few days.

LUKE
26 AUGUST

You decide to call Andy from your phone. You call him on WhatsApp so that he can't tell where you are.

"All right?"

"Where the fuck are you? Nobody's seen you for days."

"Just having some quality time — you know… "

"You dirty dog! And there was me thinkin'. Trouble is, you need to do it in your own time."

"Yeah, yeah, I'll be back later tonight. Just overslept."

"Fuckin' over-slept, did you? This isn't fuckin' Butlins. Get your arse back here. I'll be waiting at your gaff."

"It'll be late."

"I'll be here. You're lucky I'm in a good mood else, who knows, know what I mean?"

"Keep your shirt on."

Fuck, fuck, fuck.

You turn your phone off then go to the customer service desk for a flight back to London. There are no flights until tonight. You'll get in at midnight, then an hour or so from the airport will get you to your gaff by about two in the morning. While you wait for your flight, you drink. One Stella after another and then fall asleep on the flight. You sleep through the buzz of conversations in the plane among all the Brits flying home. You fall asleep on the train to central London and again on the tube. You do a u-turn to Victoria Station and leave the rucksack and suitcase in the left luggage.

You decide to take a taxi the rest of the way and hope to get a little kip on the short journey.

"Wait a minute, that address sounds like the same as somewhere there's that commotion. Affected you, did it?" The cabbie sounds excited.

"Don't know what you're talkin' 'bout, mate."

"What?" He turns to take a look at you. "You been in some sort of time-warp, have you? Everybody's talkin' about it."

"What? You talking in riddles, mate."

"The fire, of course — tallest building in the area. Some people say that it just blew up like. Google it, it's blazing like a box of flamin' matches. Never seen anything like it. People was all asleep, they was, then bouff! Imagine that."

You google and are taken in by the fire and the news videos. You don't recognise the location at first. The flames just draw you in.

"Oh fuck, fuck. Oh my God!"

The first person you think about is the pregnant woman — Cecilia.

"You all right, mate? You gone as white as a sheet. You're not going to faint, are you?"

"Pull over, pull over!" You shove the door open and chuck onto the road. Strong garlic and Stella fumes make you heave more. You slump back into the seat and wipe your mouth with the back of your hand. The driver nods, disgusted, but undoubtedly grateful you didn't puke all over his cab.

By the time you arrive, there's so much light on the inside of the building it's like daylight. You think of a flame on a gigantic candle, it's so intense, you can feel the heat from the pavement. Every now and then, you hear smashing glass and spectacular lights as small explosions are set off by the heat. You're drawn in and you duck under the police cordon. Someone stands in front of you, you ignore them and continue to stare. Your eyes are drawn up to the seventh floor and you wonder about Cecilia. Then briefly about Andy whom you assume got out as he was in your flat on the ground floor.

The bottom windows burst onto the pavement, cartwheels of colour against the dark night. Others disintegrate in the heat and spark off—more fireworks. The building seems to shift downwards. The crowd hums with each new activity.

"Yikes! The building's going to blow-up." A guy beside you in his pyjamas yells into your ear..

"Fuckin' hell! What about all the babies and old people."

You turn your phone on.

"Cecilia, I don't know if you remember me. I'm the guy you promised a job... "

"You've got to get me out of here."

"I know— "

"I can't talk right now — oh my God!... Help! Help!... Ah!" Her screams rip the lining out of your stomach. You walk down the pavement examining the faces, none are familiar. You decide to try Andy. His phone goes to voicemail straightaway. You feel awkward about leaving a message, so you text him instead.

Where are you?

You're not sure what to do next, so you cross the road and sit on the pavement, your eyes on the chaos, not really taking it in. You're more concerned about Andy. You start to think that maybe Andy called you to come back because he had a surprise waiting for you. Maybe he had something unpleasant planned — the fire saved you. The perfect solution would be for Andy to have died in the fire — as much as you hate him, you think, that's a bit harsh. But you hope so anyway.

A tall bloke sits beside you, he's blubbering his eyes out.

"Lose someone in there?"

"My girlfriend... and... "

"Sorry, mate, wish there was something I could do."

Passing car lights let you have a good look at his face, it's him. You know him.

ABI
26 AUGUST

When I woke up, I could smell like electric burning, then I fell asleep again because Kudjoe's big leg was across me, I couldn't move. Then I woke again because someone was banging on the door — it sounded like Beauty shouting. The smell was also getting stronger. I tried to wake Kudjoe. I shook him. Still he didn't wake. I was more worried about the smell because it was getting bigger and bigger and the banging on the door was louder. Maybe I had left the stove on. I finally managed to get his leg up and I rolled the other way and almost landed on the floor. I hit my head on the table beside the bed. For a minute, I was a bit dazed.

"Kudjoe!" That was funny, he wasn't even snoring.

I was now worried about the smell of burning — something was definitely burning — Beauty was still banging, but I was also worried about Kudjoe. I panicked for a moment wondering which one to check first. Then I remembered what they had said in the training, check that the area is safe first. I checked the kitchen. The stove was off and there was nothing on top, I had not used the oven that day. I even checked behind the fridge because they said that sometimes they can catch fire. The smell was getting stronger.

When I opened the door to the passage, I saw Beauty. She was telling me to get out — I was confused, it was difficult to understand what she was saying. Then she pointed at the fireman. I saw smoke coming out of her flat. I decided to go and check Kudjoe. He hadn't moved from the position I had left him in, with his leg bent over the other one. My heart was beating faster, what if he was dead? I tried to shake him again. I was shouting his name. He didn't move. I checked his pulse, there was nothing. I put my ear over his face but couldn't feel his breathing. His body was still warm. If I called the ambulance, they would want me to wait with him, I didn't want to risk my life for someone who already had stopped breathing. I started running up and down the flat, I was worried about my things that I had bought for the shop, fortunately, they were all packed in two large suitcases.

Quickly, I got out my passport and my purse and the envelope with the money that I had changed to use when I next went to Nigeria, I put them in my bag and hung it around my neck. I put on my clothes then checked outside the window. Then I thought about how I could collect the suitcases with my things from the cleaning cupboard downstairs. The cleaner had let me copy the keys. I put a cardigan on to cover my bag — isn't it they say that you shouldn't stop to collect your belongings.

Beauty was still there at Betty's door. I could see smoke coming from her flat, I wondered if I should ask her.

"Beauty?"

"Wha?"

"I just thought that – it's okay."

." I could see that she was angry with me and didn't want to speak to me, so I left. The stairwell was busy — hey! Even Lagos markets doesn't get like that. People were shouting. There was even a small fight on the stairs. People were stupid and selfish, trying to force all their luggage down the stairs. I just knew that I had to get down to the ground floor somehow before someone found my suitcases. Beauty passed me on the stairs, she ignored me. I couldn't believe that she was the one who just saved my life.

Ah, this Beauty! Always drama.

I held my bag close, then I also started to push forward. The woman in front of me turned to look at me, she was annoyed, but the people were taking too long to get down and others were coming up. I suppose they had forgotten something in their flats. Fortunately, the firemen came out on each floor. They stopped people from going up and we all started going down. It was like we were all walking to hell because some of the other floors were on fire. It seems that there were lots of different fires that broke out on each floor — the big fires were going up to the next floor and meeting the ones below. I could imagine the whole place just melting.

It took almost an hour to get outside. It took me another half an hour to find my suitcases in the dark. Fortunately, everyone was busy worrying about the fire.

Then I thought of Kudjoe again. I wondered if I should tell someone, because in Africa if you don't try to help, you can get evil spirits following you around. If Ghana was like Nigeria, Kudjoe's relatives could use juju to find out what had happened to him, and then, if they thought that I was to blame, they would fix me. My business would not do well. I didn't know his people so wondered if I should phone someone. If I phoned the ambulance, then they might want to do an enquiry and, because they can't see the body, they could actually blame me for what had happened. I didn't do anything wrong, except sleep with a married man. But everybody does it, I'm not the first one. I still couldn't decide what to do. I sat watching the fire, knowing that every minute my situation was getting worse.

Whilst I was sitting there, I saw Beauty crossing the road. She sat on the wall and watched the fire. I wished that I could go and confide in her and ask her what she thought I should do. But me and her are no longer friends, in fact, it would be looking for trouble to go and ask her, I mean, what would I say to her? Eh?

I moved closer to her, I left the suitcases behind the wall next to the flat. All those nice occasion dresses, the matching shoes and handbags, the panties. Even those earrings, if I lost them all, where would I start? Before I could stop myself, I had crossed the road and was standing there. With my suitcases. She didn't notice at first, she was far away.

"Beauty, did you speak to Okafor?"

"Why are you so concerned with Okafor?"

Eh, heh, Beauty, always suspicious.

" The thing is, I saw him going into your flat. This very afternoon — and where is he now? Did he manage to get out?"

"What? This afternoon — it can't be him. He's in Nigeria."

"He was here, it was him — unless, whilst he's away, you gave your key to someone else... "

This Beauty, she started blinking fast, trying to see if I was telling the truth.

"Why don't you call him and see. Maybe he could have left to go somewhere after I saw him."

Beauty stared at me. She thought that I was being funny.

"Why are you so worried? What do you know about this fire? And about Okafor? Tell me now."

"Eh, Beauty, I'm just trying to help. I have the same thing with Kudjoe he... "

By that time, Beauty wasn't listening to me. She phoned Okafor and left a message. Then she phoned someone in Nigeria to ask him. I couldn't make out much from that conversation, except she kept saying, surprise, surprise.

Next thing her hands were around my throat and she was screaming. Even the mad people we have at work

230

don't scream like that. She shook me, hard. And she was saying something in her language, or maybe she was speaking in tongues — who knows? If it hadn't been for the fireman, Pablo and that begging boy, I would have been dead, right now. Dead. They came and pulled her off, then they sat with her.

I decided not to stick around, maybe those demons would be back to visit her and, this time, she would really kill me. I took my suitcases and left. I thought that it was better not to think about Kudjoe and forget about Beauty too.

On the way to the cab office near the station, I thought about where I should go. Maybe I shouldn't have let Beauty see me, I mean, that I had managed to get out of the fire alive. Because I had big problems waiting for me and I was in the middle, the one who had the most to lose. First, there was Kudjoe — if they found the body, they might think that I killed him. I could imagine them asking how I had managed to save myself and leave him. I wondered what he had wanted to tell me in the morning. The second problem was Nurse Katie — I was supposed to have a meeting with her the next morning. What if they had found out something and the meeting was a trap? I thought about just going straight to the airport on the next plane to Lagos. Then I remembered my order for the dresses. They had asked me to deposit two hundred-and-fifty pounds. That's a lot of money. And then there was my deposit on the flat, they would have to give that back to me now. I wondered if Mr Patel would give it back without lots of wahala.

I eventually decided to go to my cousin in Leyton. I took a cab. The cab driver said sixty-five pounds, especially since it was that time of night. I sat in the cab office for half an hour waiting. The operator was very friendly, a man from Barbados, Raymond, I think his name was.

"What's a nice lady like you travelling with all those suitcases at this time of the night for? Did you have a fight?"

"No, Raymond — my flat is burnt down. You know about the fire?"

"Oh, goodness me. We've allocated a few cars to help people move from there — you know, those that have somewhere to go. I think we'll be able to claim back from the government or the council."

"That's very kind."

"Because you're from there, we can charge you twenty pounds — how does that sound? Just to help you out a lickle — I still have to give the driver something. He's got to feed his family."

"I can manage twenty. Thank you."

MUKAI
12 SEPTEMBER

I felt the pull towards Babel and was dreading going back to work. June eyed me suspiciously when I visited her a few days before I was due to return.

"Don't tell me, you're bored, and you want to come back earlier."

I had never heard June being sarcastic, perhaps it's the workload.

"Actually, I'm having a 'whale of a time' – June I wanted to ask…"

"What? We're already one man – one woman down. Claire is off sick with God knows what."

"But,, I'm sure you've heard what sterling work I'm doing at the temporary office."

"Yes, that's true – I have had good reports back. What exactly are you doing out there?"

I spent another ten minutes explaining my daily activities.

"So, you see, I'm vital – "

"What's that I heard about you snooping around? Asking lots of questions?"

"I'm just trying to make sure that I report any wrongdoing to the authorities, you know safeguarding, negligence blah blah."

"You don't have to recite the textbook to me. I'll tell you what I'll do. I'll extend your leave for another two weeks and then – wait, wait! You'll continue to work there for two days a week as part of your working hours and the other three will have to be back here, I'm afraid. I can't do better than that."

"Thank you, June. Can I come and give you a big kiss?"

"No thank you! Just be sure to report back on time – keep up the good work."

I had already been putting in extra hours to get some of my paperwork completed and was getting home late every evening. I noticed that Nate was always home with dinner ready. I couldn't figure him out. Especially since he was taking a great interest in my work. He would wait to have dinner with me and ask for details about my day. That evening when I got in he had a candle lit dinner.

"What's the occasion?"

"Do I need an occasion to celebrate my woman?"

"I'll just get the insulin."

"I don't get it. I'm really trying here. A little understanding would be nice."

"I'm sorry- it's just. Well, you never used to be like this. All the late nights out with your friends, now that I'm working late you've suddenly changed. What's really going on Nate?"

"Look, let's sit down and eat and I'll tell you all about it."

"Okay, what's for dinner? Not Jambalaya ??"

"Well, that's hardly a romantic meal is it? Anyway, what's wrong with Jambalaya? I thought you loved it."

"I did till I discovered that's the only meal that you can cook well."

"I can cook other things too."

"I'm ready for dinner. And to hear your news."

"I'll just get the food out. Sit."

He brought the dishes out one by one—the first course, four giant prawns marinated in garlic, butter, and lemon and grilled served with a creamy dill sauce. I dipped a prawn in the sauce and closed my eyes to relive Maputo, the small rondavel on the beach that churned out prawns and Portuguese chicken for paying guests.

"I've been thinking a lot about the future. You know just how I want to live my life and what sort of life I'd like to live."

I filled her mouth with prosecco to wash down the second prawn.

"And?"

"I've been writing a business plan with James."

Crown's an interesting place to do business.

"What sort of business?"

The sliced tomato and caper, salty and mellow, slid down my throat.

"An internet security company. With my IT skills I can develop the software. I've actually developed something for a start-up that specialises in cloud storage for small businesses. They're three weeks in and they're enjoying the experience."

"Sounds great – so who next?"

The chicken was moist and tender, I felt an irresistible desire to bite his lip.

How come I never knew that he could cook like this?

"Well we have a few other companies lined up. I'm taking a sabbatical from work to try this out. It needs my full concentration."

Ahh! We're getting to the point finally

I looked across at him, waiting for him to translate it to our lives – my tongue wrestled with the spinach that he'd wilted and not cooked the way that I'd shown him. The African way with onions and tomatoes or even peanut butter.

"I have enough saved up- I should be okay with my contribution to the flat for maybe six months or so."

I nodded and sipped my drink my teeth finally free of that piece of spinach.

"I just need to know that you're okay with that?" he said returning with the final course.

I rescued the warm chocolate as it oozed out of the lava cake, chased it with the raspberry sauce and closed my eyes. A whisper a memory - a cold night by the fire in the Nyanga Mountains swept through. I opened them.

"Is six months enough?"

"I've already been doing some projects."

The chocolate suddenly seemed too strong, too rich, too dark.

"What do you want from me Nate? Where do I fit into your world?"

"I just need you by my side, that's all."

I didn't notice what he did after that, just that the table was clear, and the dishwasher loaded. I did notice what he did when we went to bed that night. I had to think about what I wanted and if he was doing this to keep me sweet – by his side. But what came after?

When I woke the next morning, Nate had already left. He'd left a note on the pillow beside her head.

Had to leave early, client visit. How about lunch? I'll call you later.

I thought about their conversation the night before and decided that the best thing would be to sit this thing out. We'd been together for a few years. I felt too preoccupied with work to want to spend hours figuring things out with Nate. Perhaps the best thing would be to give it my hundred per cent attention once I've figured out what was going on at Babel.

Beauty took me to visit Sanjay. When we got to the shop. I hadn't taken him seriously when he said the fire had been started deliberately. I asked him to explain again. Sanjay talked about a guy who had come in one night looking for a fight.

"He got one. It carried on the next day– the Spanish guy, an Indian guy and the one who didn't live at Babel."

"But what has that got to do with anything?"

237

"Well, this guy wanted revenge – the English guy. He was always hanging around the flat and trying to find out about all of them."

"But how do you know this Sanjay? I mean you're in the shop all day."

"I offer deliveries to some of the residents – things like milk, bread, cigarettes – you know. My nephew does it a few times a week, so he sees a lot of what is happening. We knew that they were planning something, but nothing this big. My God! This is incredible, that people can hate so much."

"Can I speak to your nephew? I just want to ask him exactly what happened."

I met with his nephew. He described Andy, who he noticed coming out of the flats on quite a few occasions.

"There was nothing suspicious about his appearance; it was just the fact that after saying how much he wanted revenge on the guys that beat him – the next thing he was hanging out there."

I shrugged and left for lunch with Nate that afternoon. He had news.

"Babe, I'm excited about money coming in. It's possible that this will be ongoing business – Babe? I thought you'd be excited. You seem really distracted. What's up?"

"Sorry, Nate. I'm just drowning in all the information that I have; they just seem to be loose threads, and I'm not sure that they lead anywhere."

"Run it by me, it might help you make the links."

"Well, The shopkeeper thinks the fire was started by some shady characters that have been hanging around the block for the past few months, ever since they had a fight with some of the occupants. But he can't pinpoint any actual bad behaviour, you know. Then there's this woman, Abi, who is a 'person-of-interest' by the police; she also wanted to respond to the nursing home where she works as a carer. Apparently one of the residents sustained a serious injury, so she's mixed up in that somehow. Fortunately, the police caught up with her, before she left on a flight to Nigeria. Then there's this Beauty woman, she's from Zim. She's a bit too helpful and all in your face sort of thing, I'm not sure if she's also wrapped up in this business at the nursing home. But she seems to know a lot about the other residents. She was looking after an elderly woman in her home. We're not sure she survived– Beauty has been looking for her. but I suspect that she's hiding something, but I'm not sure what. Maybe she's here illegally, who knows? Then there's the guy who was always begging for money and suddenly has new clothes, etc. Maybe he's been tied in with the shady characters, and he was involved in starting the fire. I don't know his name, so maybe he's registered on the file. It's messy!" she said messaging her fingers hard, along her scalp and disturbing my afro.

"Why not break it down and deal with each individual at a time? But why are you getting involved with all of these people? If someone did start the fire, then things could get dangerous. I don't want you getting hurt."

"I dunno – I just feel like I'm being reeled in on a fishing line. The more I meet these people, the more I want to know about them. their lives are something else. Bestseller stuff!

I think the key is Beauty. but the problem is to get her to talk. I haven't any specific questions to ask her."

"Try and get hold of the guys first – find out which ones had the fight with this guy and see if they can give you a description of some kind. He might match up with someone the police are looking for or know of, because I bet a guy like that would be known to the police for some minor crimes."

Later that afternoon, I called Beauty for a chat.

"What was the name of the guy that you said lived on your floor?"

"Pablo."

"Do you know of any fights he might have had with anyone in the area?"

"No. I don't think that he's the fighting type. He was always helpful, especially when I had problems with Abi. He also used to do shopping for Betty sometimes. That was before I started looking after her. But, I haven't seen him for a long time. I don't know if he went back to Spain – maybe he had a fight with the girlfriend. You know how these young people are."

"Thanks Beauty, that's helpful. What about the guy you said was always begging? What's his name?"

"Ah sorry, that one I don't know him. I just used to see him. I never spoke to him."

"Okay, thanks. I've got to go. See you tomorrow."

I went back to *Mags and Fags* where Sanjay helpfully told me that the guy's name was Pablo.

"But I don't think that he was involved with starting the fire. Not that one – he's a good guy."

"Who else was he with that night?"

"Priyanuj, but I think that he moved back to India for a bit – something about family problems. I don't think he's been back."

When she I back at the office, located Pablo's name on the register. I noted that he had reported that his girlfriend died in the fire. I decided to call him and find out where that would lead to. Pablo wanted to be helpful, but he was still recovering from the loss of his girlfriend. He kept mentioning her and how he felt he'd let her down. If he hadn't abandoned her, he would have been able to get her out alive, and they would be having their baby any time now. I reassured him as best I could then asked him if he remembered the fight that he'd had in Sanjay's shop and the following day in the street.

"What has that got to do with anything? How can you ask me about that? it was such a long time ago, and how will that bring Cecilia back?"

"I'm not sure, but I think there maybe a link between the fight and the reason the fire was started."

"You mean it was arson? I'd like to find those bastards." Then he started speaking in Spanish, and I couldn't understand him.

"Pablo, any information you can give me would be helpful. I just need a description, maybe the police would be able to use that information."

"I can't remember him much – short skinny, with dark brown hair. He was wearing these check designer clothes – what you call them?"

"You mean Burberry?"

"That's the one. It's not much but I hope that it will help." He said sniffing.

"It's great Pablo. Can I call you again if I have any more questions?"

I looked doubtfully at the information that I had written on her pad. A lot of bits and pieces that didn't seem to fit together. I attended to my victim support duties and forgot about these new threads for the rest of the day. When I got home, I kept googling for updates on the fire investigation. It took a few more days of searching. I watched interviews and by chance I was listening to a discussion on the radio one morning before work. A man had phoned in to say that it was little known fact that electrical appliances have caused fires and although the problem had been solved there was a chance this could have been one of those fires.

" It is possible to adjust the wiring in the back to make them flammable." The man, Jim had said sounding very sure of himself.

" I expect they'd need to be plugged in, yah?" the host asked. "But, it's still incredible – so what you're saying is that our appliances at home could combust and cause a fire? "

"Look this was discovered a while ago — say a few years ago now. But it should have been resolved. But you never know how old some of the appliances are in those flats. I heard some of the residents have been living there a long time."

"Perhaps, a long shot then?" The host sounded like he still needed to be convinced. "Thanks for phoning in, Jim. Can anyone else back up what Jim's saying? Any thoughts? Give us a ring on…"

Bloody hell! What now?

My phone rang over the radio. It was Beauty, she sounded excited about something.

"I'll be there in ten minutes or so. You can wait for me at the office. Okay, okay."

Beauty was sitting beside my desk when I walked in. I was starting a little later that morning as Nate had asked me to accompany him to look at some office space. Beauty was bubbling over.

"You remember, this Abi? Well she had a boyfriend, I think he was someone's husband and she was having an affair with him. Look, look I don't know why I hadn't deleted these photos because me and Abi are no longer friends. But the evidence is here, I am sure the police would be interested to see it."

"Yes, I suppose they would." Mukai wondered if this was the reason that they Abi was a person of interest. "If you know that the police are looking for him, then you should go to the police station and present the information."

"I don't want them to think that maybe I had something to do with him disappearing like that. maybe I can just send them anonymously. If I go there, they'll be asking me questions also."

"But you can't withhold information, Beauty. Just go, it will be fine."

"Okay but I'll send Abi a message to let her know. I'll tell her the police asked for it."

I wondered what Abi had done to Beauty to motivate her to shop her to the police. It was a bit extreme perhaps this will unravel the mystery. I thought about how all these lives were intertwined as I watched Beauty go over to wait her turn at the police desk at the far end of the room. I decided to stand nearby to hear what Beauty would say.

"This man has been missing and I think this woman knows something. she was having an affair with him. I have pictures to prove the affair."

The police appeared to be only mildly interested in the photos. They were more concerned about crimes like theft of items, and official reports about who was missing. Beauty was neither reporting a missing person or reporting a crime. She was just accusing someone without any evidence beyond the photographs even though Beauty showed them the man's photograph in the paper. They took details and Beauty's details and Abi's phone number and told her there was probably a docket open already and they would have to wait to match it to the information held on file.

BEAUTY
SEPTEMBER

Money was getting tight. Mr Patel was taking his time about returning my deposit. The money from Liam was just enough to send a little to the kids. I was going to struggle to pay their school fees. That's when I thought about talking to Mukai, maybe she could get a little something for me to do there at the temporary office. Liam was well enough for me to leave him for a few hours, but I had to be there to get his food.

Mukai was talking on the phone when I arrived. When she had finished, I sat down in the chair and told her I needed another job. I told her how I couldn't work at the nursing home because of Liam, but I needed to live somehow. I showed her the pictures of my kids and I could see that she really understood my situation. She said they only had volunteering jobs but there were some donations that had just come in.

I managed to get some food and clothing donations and a thousand pounds. I had some savings and had difficulty getting into the account that Okafor had set up for us. All my id was in the flat when the fire started. I hadn't told his family about that account because it was ours — me and him. So, I decided to volunteer with Mukai. My first job was to trace the elderly people and help her to create a register so that their relatives could be informed. I was glad that I had that job, I could try and find Betty.

I visited all the nursing homes and asked for the names of the clients that had just moved in from Babel. I thought that I could do the job in one day, but it took time. There were small nursing homes, residential homes for the elderly and for the disabled and mental health residential homes to visit. I didn't know that there were so many. I counted twenty in the postcode areas that she had given me. I managed to visit one each day. It took so long because I had to first get the names, then go and see each one, take a photo and ask them for some details — whatever they were able to tell me.

Each day when I got back to the office, I had to help Mukai match the names against the database and then she would call the relatives to notify them and discuss what would happen next. One day when the afternoons were getting colder, we sat with a cup of tea, I told her how disappointed I was that I hadn't managed to find Betty. She tried to reassure me and I told her that I wasn't surprised that no one had come to ask about her because of the way her children had just abandoned her. She started to ask me about some of the other people in the flat.

"Between you and me, there's something fishy about this fire. It just seems odd. I can't say at the moment but I'm sure we'll find out soon enough. Perhaps if I spoke to some of the other people who lived in the flats, I could get a better picture. What do you know that can help me?"

"Well, there was Abi, Betty, Pablo and his girlfriend — think her name was Cecilia and there was this other guy who lived on the ground floor. I don't know his name. I remember him because he was always begging for change. But you know, the last few months I didn't see him that much. I think he managed to get a job somewhere because he was wearing new clothes. Then there were a few people I used to meet in the lift. Oh, yes, I remember when I first moved in, I had a fight with two black boys. I think one of them was called Dwayne, something like that."

"That's helpful. I will look out for them."

She wrote the names down and I asked her how she was going to find out about how the fire started. Then I remembered Sanjay.

"Everybody used to go to his shop to buy bread, milk and what, what."

I couldn't remember the name of the shop, but I took her there one day after we finished work. When we got there, she said she knew it and goes there every time.

ABI
SEPTEMBER

By the time I arrived at my cousin's house, it was half past three or four in the morning and she was at work. Her teenage son, Obi, answered the door after I had been ringing for about twenty minutes. He had gone quite tall since I last saw him two years ago. It took him a while to recognise me and, when he did, he took the suitcases and invited me in. There was no bedroom available, so I made myself comfortable on the sofa and tried to sleep.

I couldn't. When I closed my eyes I saw Kudjoe's face and the position that I had left him in. In my bed. My heart started pounding, I opened my eyes. There was nothing I could do about that.

I tried again.

This time I fell asleep and dreamt of Nurse Katie. Her face was red and she was shouting at me, but I couldn't hear what she was saying. I woke up sweating. I sat up and went to the kitchen for a glass of water.

I sat back on the sofa and finally managed to fall asleep sitting up. I dreamt of nothing. It was only for a few minutes, I'm sure. Next thing, someone was opening the curtains and the sun was shining on my face. I tried to sleep but I could feel someone in the room. I opened my eyes and saw my cousin sitting there at the dining room table watching me.

I smiled and she smiled back but I think she was more wondering about what had brought me to her house. The last time Femi and I had spoken and been in the same room was at our grandmother's funeral when I was given the important things that belonged to my grandmother, even though she was older. There had been a big, big fight. I won because she is physically weak. Maybe she didn't get enough food when she was growing up, but me, I know I was a bouncing baby with plenty of food.

She greeted me eventually and asked the necessary questions.

"Eh huh," she said.

I knew then she was expecting me to tell her why I was there sleeping on her leather couch, using her silk cushions for my oily head. There was even a dark mark on one of them.

"My sister, wo. My flat burnt down in the middle of the night — so I knew that you would not turn me away and that you will give me somewhere to stay for a few days."

"Of course." I could see that she wasn't feeling generous. "Eh he, you mean that fire in west London? You mean that was where you were living? The place that you never welcomed me or my children?"

I felt foolish maybe because, at that time, I needed her more than she needed me. But her face was hard, wo. I stood up and went to hug her. I was crying now, tears just falling. She turned and left the room. I sat down and thought for a long moment. I heard the children talking and laughing upstairs, then the noises moved to the kitchen. I badly needed a shower, but I was afraid to move.

Siji, her husband, came downstairs to save me. He sat with me and enquired about my health and my husband. As if he didn't know that we were no longer together. I suppose that Femi had chosen not to tell him because nobody in our village had ever left a husband. I decided to play along.

"Everybody is fine. In fact, I am going home in the next few days." In that moment, I decided that my time in England had come to an end, it was time to finish what I had started. I didn't have much to do on the house where I would live and, over the next few days, I could buy the fittings and furniture that I wanted. Somehow, it would have to work.

I felt free after that — no more Nurse Katie, no worrying about Kudjoe and no pressure from Beauty.

When Femi went to bed, I had a shower and went out. I collected my dresses, went to B & Q for my fittings and ordered furniture to be delivered to the shipping company. That was the advantage I had from living a simple life — I had saved quite a lot of money, still had some left in savings and there was also my pension which would be ready for me later. I bought my ticket to Lagos.

I was free.

I was finishing my packing when my mobile rang. It was a withheld number. I decided to ignore it, I wasn't expecting any calls. When it went to voicemail, I checked.

This is a message for Abi, it's Nurse Katie from Sunset Lodge. Please can you call me? You were supposed to be at work today.

I rang the agency and told them about the fire. I wanted to keep on their good side as, you never know, I might need them someday. Life can be funny. They sympathised with me and asked me to provide a new address, but they said that I needed to get in touch with Nurse Katie. I persuaded them to call her on my behalf. I did a lot of crying and some fast breathing. I had seen enough panic attacks. They sympathised and then agreed that it must be very traumatic for me.

I made up my mind not to call Nurse Katie. She would insist that I come into work and then things would get out of control. I would have to leave. I took out my phone and checked the flight details.

I decided to buy some groceries for my cousin's house to say thank you for looking after me. I went first to the butcher and then to the big Tescott. The bags were too heavy, so I called for a cab. It was a short distance that cost about ten pounds. I put my bags in the boot and got in the back. I nearly fainted when I saw the driver's face in the mirror.

"Eh, my sister, how are you?"

"I'm fine, Brother Kwake, how is the family?"

"Well, thank you."

"Praise God!"

"I've just started work today. You know, I've been spending time with my sister. You know Kudjoe didn't come home last night. My sister is so worried. If I knew where you lived, I would have come there to check."

"Me? Why would you come to check with me?"

I looked back at him hard in the mirror.

"You can pretend if you like, my sister, but the truth always comes out in the end."

I was starting to feel uncomfortable as he was driving and I wished I hadn't given the operator the full address. My mobile rang again, suddenly everyone was calling me. It was someone from work, I decided not to answer it. I could feel Kwake's eyes watching me in the mirror.

"You no go answer?"

"It's the agency — I don't want to work."

The phone stopped ringing and then started ringing again immediately after.

Hey, things were getting scary.

I decided that, after he dropped me off, I would take another cab to the airport and wait there until my flight. I could see him watching which house I went to. Femi was at work and it was just the kids at home. I gave them the shopping to put away and gave them ten pounds each. I called for a taxi, this time a different company. I had no time to shower or change my clothes.

Obi helped me take the suitcases out to the front door. It was nearly six o clock and the taxi hadn't arrived yet. Maybe there was a lot of traffic, I didn't know. I hoped the

taxi arrived before Femi or her husband returned home —
they would have too many questions and delay me. My
flight was at eleven p.m.

I stood outside waiting and checking my phone. I saw
a car arrive with about five women. I could tell that they
were Ghanaian because they were speaking in what
sounded a bit like Twi. I had heard Kudjoe speaking it on
the phone to his people. It was only when I saw them
checking the house numbers, that I realised that they were
looking for Femi's house, Kwake must have told them.
Maybe if I pretended I was Femi, I would be able to get
away. I didn't know at that time what they might be
capable of doing. One of them was quite big.

They stopped in front of Femi's house. I blocked their
entrance.

"Can I help you?"

The shortest one answered. She was a very beautiful
woman with dark smooth skin.

"We're looking for my husband — Kudjoe. I was told
that I might be able to find him here."

"There's no one here by that name. You can tell
whoever told you that they were wrong."

A tall, big one — about Beauty's size, with a loud
voice, came from the back.

"Who are you?"

"What do you need my name for? If you don't leave
now, I'll have to call police."

"We don't care about the police, we are helping them
with their enquiries to find a missing person."

"Well, you can't come in." I decided not to move. I could have got away with it if it wasn't for Obi who came out of the house.

"Auntie Abi, I heard shouting, are you all right?"

"Eh eh, Abi, so you are Abi!" It was the oldest one in the group. She grabbed me by the collar and they all pushed me to the ground. Then Kudjoe's wife pushed her way into the house, she was followed by three other women. The other two stayed to hold me down.

The taxi arrived and I could see that the driver was confused about what he should do. He needed his money.

There was a lot of shouting and, every time I tried to speak, I was slapped hard around the head. It must have been Obi, that called for help. I could just see his frightened face peeping from the window.

The next thing I knew, I was sitting at the police station with my suitcases. They had separated me from those women who had been taken to a private room. I sat waiting in the corridor wondering how this would work out. Then a policewoman took me into the interview room and left me there.

It was scary. My pants felt wet, but this was not the time to ask for the toilet. I wished I had someone to call to be with me. But they had taken my phone, my bag and, of course, the money. My suitcases were somewhere inside the police station behind the desk. I hoped that they would keep my things safe.

For the next hour, I cried. Then I felt angry with Kudjoe, if it wasn't for him, I wouldn't be in this situation.

I wondered what that Ghana woman had told them about me. About Kudjoe. My tummy grumbled and I wished I could be back in my flat eating rice and chicken. I heard something knock on the window to my right and wondered if they could see me. Maybe they were watching me to see if I looked guilty. That's when I stopped crying. I wiped my eyes with my sleeve and sniffed back my runny nose.

When maybe an hour had passed, two policemen came in. They confirmed my name and then sat down.

"This interview is being recorded and may be given in evidence if your case is brought to trial, we are interview room twelve at Leytonstone Police Station, the date is 30 August... "

I didn't hear the rest because my heart was beating so loud — this is what they said on tv before they threw someone in prison. I just heard the last bit.

"I'm Detective Inspector Amy Williamson and this is Detective Sergeant Avi Ahuja. Please state your full name and date of birth."

After I had told them what they wanted to know, the woman carried on talking.

"May I call you Abiola?" The policewoman asked then she looked at the brown file that she was carrying. She made sure that I could see that there were a lot of papers inside it.

"Yes." I don't know why I was whispering.

"Pardon, could you speak up please." She was mean. The blonde ones were always like this — hard. And she was so young, I couldn't imagine what she would be like when she grew old.

"Don't be scared, we're here to help you." I suppose they brought this Indian one in because of this diversity thing. I looked at his turban. But he talked as if he was talking to a small child, so it wasn't working.

"Yes," I almost shouted, he was irritating me.

"She's certainly got a voice on her, hasn't she?" She turned to him as if they were mocking me. I kept telling myself to stay calm.

" I see here you refused a lawyer?"

"No one asked me — anyway, I thought I was here to make a statement — I was attacked by those Ghana women."

"You did, did you?" She was making wrinkles on her face by making those cruel faces.

"You're here for a much more serious reason — didn't anyone tell you?"

"No one has told me anything." I wiped my face with my sleeve. "I want a lawyer. I don't know what you people are planning here."

I knew that they would have to stop the interview. They brought me my phone so that I could look for a number of my pastor so that he could ask one of the lawyers from church to come as soon as possible. In the meantime, I was left in that room. No food, no water, nothing. I was scared to ask for even water in case they told me that it was not a hotel.

Then the Indian one came back again, to add some diversity.

"Listen, Abi. These are serious charges. If you haven't got a lawyer, we can get you a duty solicitor."

"I have my own lawyer coming."

He kept talking, but I stopped listening, wo. He saw that what he was trying was not working. So, he left. Then he came back with a cup of tea. I drank it — at least it was something. I waited and, after a long time, the door opened again. This time it was Brother Joe. I had heard that he had experience in dealing with the police.

"Ah! Sister Abi. How are you? What happened for you to be in this place?"

I told him about the fight.

"It wasn't really a fight — I was beaten by those women. Also, I will lose my flight tonight. I'm supposed to be leaving for Lagos tonight."

"But that is not what I heard. They are saying that you know something about Brother Kudjoe, he has been missing from home. The police have opened a docket — a missing person file. You can just forget about that flight, you won't be travelling tonight because you are facing an assault charge."

"Oh, I can't afford to lose that flight. I don't know why they are accusing me — I don't know anything about the missing person."

"Like I said, the police won't allow you to leave whilst this docket is open. You'll be lucky if they let you out of the police station. This is serious — why can't you understand? The wife says that she has been informed by a reliable source that the two of you were together."

I opened my mouth to respond. But he interrupted me.

"Please, I want the truth now. If you want me to help you — oh, this is a big mess, Sister Abi."

"I am telling the truth."

"The police have your phone — they are going through it now. If there have been any calls or messages they will discover the nature of your relationship with him — never mind, if you have deleted anything. Truth, please."

"Well, he used to visit me."

"Ah ha, why was he visiting you?"

"He just came to eat with me."

"Oh, my sister, you are talking to an African brother, there is no way that he would come just to eat food — unless you mean some other... ?'"

I looked at the ceiling, then at the floor, then I looked at his hands.

"Oh! We don't have much time, my sister. Please just tell me everything."

"We were just friends." I could imagine if I told him everything then they would know at church — it would be bad.

"Okay, if that is what you say, then I have to respect your decision to withhold information from me."

I looked down. He got up and knocked on the door so that they would let him out. He returned a few minutes later with the police officers from earlier. They all sat down and they repeated everything they had said earlier after they turned on the tape recorder.

"So, what happened tonight?" It was Blondie, I suppose she would do most of the talking. Whilst I explained, the turban one was just looking at me and then at Brother Joe as if he was trying to measure how good he was. I told them about what had happened and the fact that I thought that Brother Kwake told them where to find me. I was getting more and more uncomfortable because Blondie kept repeating the last few words that I said, as if she couldn't believe what she was hearing.

"So, why do you think they attacked you?"

"I think they got wrong information."

When I finished talking, she opened her folder and she took out some pictures.

"Are you sure you had nothing to do with this man?"

Blondie pulled one of the pictures from the folder, "Who is that?"

The picture was of me and Kudjoe enjoying ourselves at Gold Coast. He had his arm around my waist. I remembered that picture, Beauty had taken it that night when we were still friends. I could feel Brother Joe's eyes killing me from next to me.

"That's me, of course."

"And who is that you were with?"

"Yes, that is Brother Kudjoe."

"You look quite cosy — do you do this with men that you don't know?" Blondie. Her eyes looking like they could cut mine.

259

"You can just tell us if it was one time only. I mean was he paying you — you know!"

"I am not a prostitute! I work hard as a carer." I didn't mean to shout, but they were just taking liberties. Brother Joe patted my hand to calm me down.

"Sir, please ask your client not to raise her voice." Blondie liked to be in charge.

"Abi, eh, just calm down." He was trying to make his voice soft, but I could tell he was mad about that picture.

"Did you have sex with this man? I mean, it looks like you were at a club or party or something. Sometimes people have a little too much to drink and end up going home together. It's nothing to be ashamed of, we're all adults." Turban was stroking his beard trying to look wise.

"I didn't drink that night."

"So, you do remember this night? Who took the photo?"

"I don't remember."

They went on and on with the questions. I decided not to change my story. Me and Kudjoe were just friends. Unless they spoke to Beauty, they wouldn't have any evidence. There was no longer any link between me and Beauty so they would not find out. It was late. I was tired. I think Brother Joe noticed.

"I think my client needs a rest. We can resume at a later date when you have evidence that she was involved in the disappearance of this man. As for the assault charge — my client was attacked. By four women, no less. You can see the bump on her head and there is bruising around her eye. I will be advising my client to press assault charges against these women."

"We would advise you not to leave the country — I see here that you have a ticket to Nigeria. You won't be going just yet. We will be holding your passport as well as your phone. You must report to the police station twice a week. We will advise you of any new evidence. In the meantime, you are free to go. Please provide an address where you will be staying. However, if we discover that you have been lying to us, we will arrest you for lying to the police." I don't need to tell you that was Blondie saying that.

Brother Joe gave his address and said that I would be staying with him. But when we got outside, it was another story.

"You can only stay tonight whilst you find something permanent, then you need to give the address to the police." I tried to argue my side, where was I to go? My cousin had arrived home in the middle of the chaos and she had pointed her lip at me, to show me how disgusted she was. Everyone in her family now thought that I was a bitch who cheated on my husband with someone else's husband. My flat at Babel no longer existed. He encouraged me to go back there so that I could be reallocated a new flat.

The next day, Brother Joe offered me a lift back as he said that he could help me get allocated something quick, quick. When we got there, he told the social worker that I am 'a person of interest' in ongoing police enquiries and that if they could not issue me with a new address, immediately, I might have to be put in a cell.

When we arrived, there was even worse chaos than I'd seen at Femi's house with those Ghana women. People in dirty clothes sitting along the pavement opposite looking like they had always lived there. Other people were arriving with boxes and bags full of donations; tinned food, clothing and blankets. The bossy ones were trying to organise. We went into the temporary offices that they were using to organise. I had to give my details to this woman. There was something about her that reminded me of Beauty.

"Hi, I'm Mukai."

"I'm Abi — where are you from, Mukai?"

"West London, just a few miles from here."

"But Mukai is not an English name, is it?"

"Yah — well, it's Shona — you know, Zimbabwe?"

These people are everywhere — they are too westernised. Look at her.

I don't know if she knew what I was thinking but she carried on reassuring me in a gentle voice. She asked me questions and showed that she really cared. The way they taught us in training at the agency. I started to relax whilst she was talking.

Then this noise started bubbling out of me, my face was wet. Some people stopped to look, Mukai comforted me and gave me tissues. I had never felt like this before.

Afterwards, I was glad that I cried because I felt better. But at the same time, I realised that my situation hadn't changed so I felt bad again. I was told that I might be rehoused later that day. They could send me anywhere. I thought that perhaps I could accept anything until this case was over. Then I would definitely leave for Nigeria. For good.

I sat in the sun outside waiting and wondering what I should be doing in the meantime. Then it was as if I had just suddenly woken up from a bad dream and fallen into a much worse one. I had left my suitcases in the corner whilst I spoke to Mukai — they were gone. All three of them.

I used the tissue from the tears to try to keep my face dry, whilst I searched the area. Then a man walked past holding up one of the occasion dresses for my shop.

"Excuse me, where did you get that dress from?"

"From the church — they're handing out brand new dresses. I think one of the shops must have donated them. Imagine how generous some people can be."

"It's mine, you must give it back."

"No, no, you don't understand how it works — you have to go and line up with everybody else and get your own."

I tried to grab the dress, but my finger got stuck in the lace on the sleeves. I felt the tear as if someone was cutting my stomach.

"Look what you've done — my wife can't wear that."

"It's you that doesn't understand — that dress came from my suitcase of clothes for my shop — do I look like I can afford to donate?"

The man looked at me, he blinked and I knew he didn't believe me.

"Where did you get it?" I saw no point in trying to keep that dress.

He pointed up the road to the Church.

"St Peter's."

Normally, I'm not the sort of person that does a lot of running. But that day I ran. It wasn't very fast, but it was better than walking.

The queue in the church had grown long with women wanting new dresses and bras and panties — from my suitcases. I pushed my way in and ignored those people that were telling me to get to the back of the queue. You know how British it is to wait in the queue even when people are stealing your things.

I was out of breath when I got to the front — there was a woman really enjoying handing out the clothes. Fortunately, they had only managed to open one suitcase, the other two were locked but someone was trying to force one of them open with a hair clip.

"Excuse me — these are my things. Please you! Stop breaking the lock on my suitcase."

The woman who was handing out my dresses looked me up and down. I could see her eyes measuring me.

"I don't believe you." Her small, hard eyes challenged me.

I took the keys out of my bag and opened one of the suitcases.

"Yes, these are mine!" I shouted, making my eyes hard like hers. "Get off, all of you and give me back my things."

"Oh! but you have more than enough. Think of all these poor people… "

"Do I look like social welfare? Am I the benefits office? These are for my shop in Nigeria — I have worked twelve-hour shifts to buy these things. If you don't give back all my dresses, I'm going to call the police." For that moment, I chose to forget about the fact that I was a person of interest to the police.

I threw off my top and I was feeling mad. I wanted anyone there to challenge me. They were quiet. And as if by magic, that girl — Mukai came forward.

"Abi, put your top back on. Everybody, please put her things back and you need to step away."

"Who are you?" The hard-eyed woman asked her.

"I am Abi's social worker — we don't want to raise a safeguarding issue here. If these things belong to her, you have no right to distribute them."

"So, you're not even sure that they are her belongings. So how can you judge?"

"She's just proved that they're hers by opening the suitcase. Abi, do you have a list of everything?"

"Yes, I do." I was trying to close my blouse but had discovered a button missing so I opened the blue suitcase and removed a casual top and squeezed myself into it. By that time, some of the women began to feel afraid that I would come after them — my wig had moved to the side and the fringe was hanging over my left ear.

Mukai went 'round collecting the clothes from those that had brought them back, then she folded them and put them into the suitcase. The hard-eyed woman watched. She was quite cross by that time.

We took my suitcases back to the office where I had met Mukai and she explained that they had found a bed and breakfast for me. Then she said that, since she was going home, she could give me and my suitcases a lift there.

All the way there I cried. She comforted me.

"It's going to be all right." That's all she said.

After we arrived at my new place, she looked around and then she sat down on the bed and smiled at me. She was very smart, that Mukai. She knew that I was holding back. I couldn't tell her anything.

"I don't know what to do now. I just want to get back to Nigeria."

"Well, you just need to be patient. I'm sure whatever this problem you have with the police will soon be solved."

She smiled.

"Abi, is there anything else you need to tell me? I might be able to help."

"There's nothing to tell… "

I got up and turned the kettle on. I opened the window next to the table where the kettle was sitting and looked outside. She refused the tea. Then I was left to the small room, tiny bed and my secrets staring at me in the corner.

MUKAI
SEPTEMBER 23

I was always analysing new information and wondering what to do next and which hat to wear when talking to different people. Like the day I went to the police station.

I got fed up of waiting in the stuffy waiting room but after I phoned, someone came to collect me. We went up some stairs to an open space with numerous, occupied desks, then we turned into an office with large windows. When I sat down, I got a good look at my guide while he recovered his breath. He gave a big cough, evidence of a heavy smoking habit, and his belly quivered.

"Excuse me!" he said, and his hand shot up from his mouth to push the beads of sweat backwards into his grey, receding hairline. I wondered about his choice of blue and red patterned tie with a green and yellow checked shirt. "Birthday present from the kids," he said by way of explanation. I smiled obligingly.

"So, you said that you have some important evidence regarding the fire – at Babel?"

"Yes- "

"Before you go on, can I just ask you what your role is at the temporary relief office?"

I told him most of what I did, but I decided not to declare my role as a social worker for the moment.

"Go on! What have you got then?"

I gave him everything I had up to that point. I emphasised what Beauty had told me about her flat being one of the starting points for the fire, and that she had purchased her fridge down the road from the flats.

"I've got the names and numbers here," I said, and I produced my blue notebook from my bag.

"You say that this woman was referred there by this guy Luke, who also lived at the flat?"

"Yes, I heard he lived on the ground floor."

" Did he also work at the electrical shop?"

. "I don't think Luke worked there, according to Beauty, he was being paid a commission to refer clients there – she said that she overheard a conversation between Luke and this guy – Brian. Besides the latest report is that they think the fire could have been caused by the electrical appliances

"The sixty-four-dollar question is what makes you think that this caused the fire? We haven't even got the report yet from the investigators."

"Right there," he said jabbing a finger towards me, "It's great that the public come forward with bits of information, like you've done today– thank you. We're a bit limited on what we can investigate it would help if we had a bit more to go on. I can tell you that right now we are investigating some other possible causes"

"But, how else would the fire have started when she wasn't in the flat? Even if her boyfriend was there – neither of them smoke."

"What exactly is your interest in all of this?"

"To be honest, from the beginning I felt sorry for all the victims. Once I was involved, I started to discover things - I'd like everyone to get justice."

"I'm not so sure that it's arson – nothing's pointing that way at the moment. But, it's not to say that we don't value this information. I'd be very interested to get any more information from you. Just call me directly."

He handed over his card with a smile. And just like that, I was dismissed. I didn't try to hide the disappointment on my face. He didn't even ask for Luke's details. I'd have to work on Luke myself.

One the way back I stopped at a coffee shop and treated myself to a mid-morning hot blueberry muffin. I bit into it and eyed the blue gluey liquid that oozed out and thought about how to entice Luke to the area. Maybe if he thought...

Hi Luke, I just thought you should know that Brian is under police investigation. It might be a good idea for you to come and tell your side of the story. Especially if you're not involved. Mukai, social worker.

I watched the message disappear into the stratosphere.

I kept an eye on my phone while I finished the coffee, and then, on an impulse, passed by the electrical shop to see if it was open. I was worried Brian might close the shop if he knew there was any suspicion. The shutters were up allowing a view of the goods in the window, I moved to the door and pushed it before noticing the closed sign above my head. As I was turning away, a movement at the back of the shop caught my eye. The daylight that filtered from an open door at the back outlined a bulky figure. I banged against the glass until someone came forward. I had no idea what I was going to say to the menacing bulk that was bumping towards the door.

"Yes?"

"I'm looking for Brian."

"What do you want him for?"

"I was referred by Andy – he said that you could give me a good deal on a fridge. I'm desperate."

"We're closed – come back tomorrow."

"Are you..."

The door closed, and I swallowed the air that it pushed my way.

There was nothing left to do but go and wait back at the office for Luke to respond, and for the next day so that I could go back to the shop. Beauty passed by to catch up on the latest. I asked her for a description of Brian.

"He must be the guy that I saw at the shop."

"If you're going back there, I can come with you and show you which fridge I bought. I can even tell you which one is this Brian man."

We arranged to visit Brian the following morning. Beauty kept talking about how evil Abi was because she allowed her Okofor to die in the fire. Which led me to interview Abi. When I tried to get some different information Beauty just kept coming back to the night of the fire.

I found the temporary number Abi had left.

"Abi, did you find your phone? Oh, that's a pity. I'm sure you had a lot of your information and contacts in there. So how are things? Have you settled in yet? So, when do you leave for Nigeria? Have you been in touch with that nurse – what do you call her again?"

Abi was not forth coming with any information, another dead end. But at the very least I think I had reassured Abi of my concern for her. In time, she might come forward.

I answered a call from Nate

"Hey, what's up? Making any progress?" He always sounded so bright and breezy. Everything must have been going well in his part of the world. I felt a pang of envy.

"I'm just feeling a little discouraged – stalemate."

"Be patient – Rome and all that. I called to tell you that we've been invited round to James' house tonight to meet his new babe."

I groaned inwardly, I liked James, quite a lot actually, but he had a penchant for vacuous women that I could never connect with. It made it awkward as James was keen for my approval.

"Okay, I'll be home at six and we can walk round together."

At a quarter to eight we stood in the still evening on James' doorstep waiting for him to answer the doorbell. The day was suspended in a calm rosy glow, before twilight seeped in. I had changed several times unable to decide what to wear because of the time of year. I eventually chose a royal blue, off-the-shoulder maxi in jersey with puffed sleeves. I remembered last summer when I had looked like a blue sausage because it was so snug.

The door opened and once more I admired the entrance. The walls and ceiling were in an inviting shade of grey blue, and the floor, with its complex geometric blue, brown and black tiles led to the open plan kitchen dinner at the back. James' new girlfriend hadn't arrived yet.

We sat under the brise-soleil commenting on how the dying sunlight covered the space with zebra shadows.

"Tell us about your latest – what does she do?" I turned the bottle of perfectly chilled rose around so that I could read the label. "Mmm good stuff !"

"She can tell you herself," he said, getting up to answer the doorbell.

Me and Nate grimaced at each other. I rolled my eyes and put my hands together in a mock prayer. We stared, as a tall mixed-race woman walked in with the scent of summer. She smiled and extended a hand with blunt, chipped purple fingernails.

"Kenya!" she said by way of introduction, then wafted back into the kitchen in search of James.

The rest of the evening was dominated by James' obsession with civil rights and Marxism. Kenya merely nodded and spoke at twenty words for the first half of the evening. She seemed to pick her words carefully, but it was hard to discern her personality.

"James can be a bit – extra can't he?" I tried, when the guys had moved to the braai area.

"He's alright," Kenya responded.

"Ndebele?" I asked hoping I could still differentiate between the second largest ethnic grouping of Zimbabwe and South Africa.

"Yes, you must be Shona."

Kenya seemed to relax after finding out that I was also from Zim. We started talking about work. She was a graphic designer but had a physics degree from Imperial College. The comparisons that Kenya made between physics and graphic design made me think about connections between people, Luke and Pablo, Abi and Beauty, Beauty and Betty. Beauty and Luke. There was a thread or person that had laid the foundation for this disaster. The common denominator was Luke. Could he also be linked to the fire? He seemed to be reluctant to come in even before I had told him about the visit by the two goons.

When I mentioned that I was helping the Babel victims, Kenya was quite interested. She said she passed the block everyday on her jog in the early hours of the morning and sometimes at night.

"I always wondered about the people that lived there. There's this one guy that I see quite often, only thing is that each time I see him, he's driving a different car. Nothing posh, just the usual Honda, Vauxhall – you know that kind of car. I wondered whether he was a car dealer or maybe something else? - because I've never seen him with the same car. Are there some hardcore crims living there?"

"I wouldn't say so – you wouldn't happen to remember what this guy looked like?"

Kenya described him but to be honest it could have been any white male under thirty. It's only when she said that one day he had forgotten to close his windows and he ran back inside and she saw him closing a window on the ground floor, that I realised that he might be the elusive Luke. I wondered, for the millionth time, what he was dealing in.

The next day I called the local surgeries to locate Luke's GP, and using my official job title, asked for his next of kin. I was given the details of his mum, which included her house number. Then I reluctantly phoned an old contact at the benefits office.

"Eh, so you have decided to call me *he he*. I knew you would look for me eventually. When can I see you? Tonight?"

A"Hello Harrison, it's been a long time, how are you?"

"Well, I'm still single."

"Harrison, I need a favour, please."

"As long as it doesn't involve sacrificing our firstborn son."

I explained about my involvement with the relief office and the register that I had created. He happily provided evidence from Luke's file. I discovered the child support payments that he was making and tracked them back to about four years earlier.

"When can I come and take you out? We can go anywhere you like – Nandos, Pizza Hut - you name it."

"Thank you, Harrison. I can't go out with you, I already told you I have a boyfriend."

"Well, he's just a boyfriend – if he really loved you he would have married you by now – beautiful, sexy woman like you. He is just…"

"Harrison, we got engaged."

"Engaged is not married, he can still go off and leave you – I would marry you tomorrow if you just gave me a chance."

"Thank you, Harrison – but I love him." As I said the words, I suddenly realised that I really did love Nate. A lot.

"Oh really – I am very disappointed. If you ever stop loving him – I'll be here waiting."

"Thank you, I'll remember that."

After I'd put the phone down, I checked the information that Harrison had provided. The payments were being made to a woman named Mel, presumably the mother of his child. Harrison even managed an address for her. Beauty arrived while I was wondering what to do with all this information. Beauty sat watching a video on her phone. I stared at her for a moment.

"CCTV! Why didn't I think of it earlier?"

Beauty looked up from her phone startled and removed her headphones.

"No, I'm watching a video – *Bustop TV*. They are so funny these people... "

"I mean I need to get some footage for CCTV in the area. Maybe the last three or four months. "

"Okofor's cousin works for a security company, he would know how to get hold of CCTV. But it would be a problem asking him for this because I haven't been in touch with the family since -"

"Oh but, Beauty you could tell them you want to find out why he didn't wake up and leave the building. I mean you could say that you wanted to see if he looked alright, if he had bought any booze, things like that – please Beauty, it's important."

"But his family didn't know that he used to drink. They are church people."

"Okay, but why not think about it while we go and visit that Brian."

"Oh yes, we still have to go there – maybe you could also see Brian and them on the CCTV. I don't feel like going anymore. I just don't want to do anything that will remind me of Okofor, right now."

It took an hour or so to persuade Beauty. I told her that the investigation couldn't go on without her. An hour and a half later, we were standing outside the shop, the man Beauty confirmed was Brian let us in. He glared at us and made us walk under his arm as he held the door open. Neither of us wanted to be that close to him. I coughed when the cigarette smoke blew in my face, then sneezed after the dust I disturbed on top of a small fridge tickled my nostrils.

"Luke referred you, did he? When was that then?"

I hesitated then said, last week.

"Funny, but we've been looking for him. How comes he phoned you then?"

"Well, actually I just said last week but what I mean is my friend here, bought a fridge from you a few weeks ago and she recommended it last week. She said that I should say Luke referred me so that I could get a good deal. I haven't actually spoken to Luke – I haven't even met him."

"Is that right is it?" He looked back suspiciously, then at Beauty, "Oh yes, I remember you. I suppose you'll also be wanting a new fridge now. I'll give you a discount.

"What size fridge you looking for?" He asked leading the way to the nearest wall that was barely visible because of the fridges.

I looked at Beauty willing her to speak up.

"Which is the one that you bought again?"

One of the men from the back came closer to take a look at us. He nodded at Brian as if urging him on. Then he returned to his conversation outside. I wasn't sure but I thought one of the guys looked like Uriah's brother.

"Electric Ice – this one" Beauty reached over to open the fridge next to Brian.

"We're not selling that one anymore. You'll have to take something else, what about this Brice model? It's the same size and I can give it to you twenty quid cheaper."

"I want this one," I insisted, pointing at the one Beauty had just opened.

"No can do. Tell you what, I can do the other one for forty-five pounds cheaper. And I can deliver it today."

"That's okay, I'll look for it somewhere else."

"You won't find it, and besides you won't get a better deal than the one I'm offering you right now."

"Thanks, but no thanks," I said and turned to leave with Beauty close behind.

Brian followed us to the door and when we got there he muttered under his breath, "Bloody waste of time!" and slammed the shutters shut. We didn't dare turn around.

We hurried back to the office. We sat in silence for a few minutes checking the door to make sure that none of the guys had followed us back. After a cup of tea, I persuaded Beauty to phone Okorfor's cousin, Henry, on speaker phone. The call went much better than we expected. Henry was apologetic about not being in touch with Beauty. It had been a terrible loss. They were all trying to make sense of what happened ... if he hadn't been in such a rush ... yes, the surprise thing that he was trying to pull off backfired badly.

"It was such a loss. He was such a good, good man. That day, he wanted to surprise you when you came from work. Such a shame" Then he was quiet while Beauty explained the reason for the call.

"I understand that you would want to get closure – as they say. But I can't get hold of those things. You can make a request from the company that owns it. Just go around the area and check, especially outside the local shops. They will have one on the estates which the council share with the police, I don't think they'll give you those because they are probably still investigating the cause of the fire. But the shop owners can let you have a look."

Before he even finished his last sentence, I had already collected my handbag and indicated for Beauty to follow me. When we got to *Mags and Fags*, I checked outside the shop for cameras. Sanjay was busy with a customer so we had to wait for the elderly man to pack his shopping into the blue plastic bags that Sanjay had given him. Beauty decided to speed things up a bit and stuffed some of the shopping into one of the bags. The man was annoyed and grabbed the bag back. I pulled Beauty's arm to make her step away from the counter.

Sanjay gave us the file from the end of July.

"Make sure you don't let anyone know that I let you watch them – you know, data protection."

Beauty was unable to identify most of the shoppers that had walked into the shop for the past thirty days. Which was really annoying as it took hours to get through them and she had to take frequent breaks to check on Liam. I made an appearance at the office and filed a little paperwork. When the last tape squiggled to the end we went out to the front of the shop.

"Nothing?" Sanjay asked.

"What about the ones from the front, outside?"

"I don't think it'll help much – I usually turn it off during the day."

This camera had swung around the area and picked up movement across the road. On some of the night film Beauty recognised Luke arriving home in the early hours of the morning. Judging from the earlier videos, his appearance had become a lot smarter – no designer clothes, but new, nonetheless. I noted the dates and times. In the last few minutes of the tape, Luke was talking to someone in a car that stopped just outside the front entrance of Babel. The other person did not alight the vehicle and after about ten minutes the car pulled away, did a u-turn and continued back down the road in the direction it had come. For a few seconds, the number plate was visible, we replayed the video scrutinising the screen until they we were able to see part of the number plate. We guessed the last three characters based on the blurry images.

Sanjay had a relative who had a friend who worked at the DVLA, and he promised to pass on some information about the registration number. On the way back to the office, I thought about the progress of the investigation. Three days later, we had nothing much to show for it. While I waited for Luke to respond, for the information on the number plate, and for Abi to loosen up, I chose to concentrate on the sightings of Luke, hoping that would yield better results.

MUKAI
4 OCTOBER

I thought about Luke as I cut the fat off the bacon, thinking about how he had been stripped of all his layers of secrets. I wondered about the legal process as I twirled it around asparagus spears making sure not to leave any green space. I thought about the blanks in Luke's story. Then my mind switched to Abi as I laid the asparagus in the baking tray, ready for the oven.

I washed a rib-eye steak with lemon water then rolled it in smashed ginger and garlic and a dash of cinnamon and sprinkled it liberally with salt and pepper. Beauty had been helpful, I thought, as I prodded meat with a spoon making it drunk with juice. Twenty minutes later, I rested the steak in the marinade, ready for the pan.

I had at least an hour before Nate would be back. I made a creamy balsamic vinaigrette with the last of the Dijon mustard and opened a new jar of grainy mustard. I shook them vigorously in a jar with balsamic vinegar and olive oil. How did all these people live together in one block of flats? So, Beauty and Abi started out as friends and they fell out over, what sounds like, a trivial matter. Abi's in a bit of a mess with that whole affair with the married man — she must feel awful — and to cap it all, Beauty blames Abi for her man perishing in the fire.

I washed and cut the romaine lettuce and added sweet peppers, strawberries, red onion and avocado into a large salad bowl. Then Betty, what a way to die, I mean, we still haven't managed to find her so she must be dead. She seemed to have a miserable existence sitting in that chair all day, waiting for God-knows-what. I was about to make the raspberry tiramisu when Nate arrived.

"I was just thinking about all these people that I got to meet in Babel. That guy was absolutely heartbroken. I think he's taking a year out in Spain so that he can heal a bit. And, of course, Luke is going to end up doing sometime — he's so young. I'm glad I don't know if I was really any help to any of them. Or maybe they think I've made things worse for them, who knows? How was your day?"

He watched me whisk the egg and sugar over a pot of simmering water.

"It's been a tricky day today. Everything went wrong for that new customer that we signed up the other day. Remember the one I told you about? I thought we were going to lose them. They're just hanging on by a thread, and if James and I don't have this sorted and running smoothly by the end of the , we're toast. We really need the business."

"Aww! I'm sorry to hear that." I brushed his lips with mine and immediately turned back to my mixture which was well-blended but slightly runny. I added the mascarpone and thick cream and, pleased with the peaks, I set the mixture aside.

"So, what can you do to resolve that? Dinner will be ready when you are."

"What's the occasion?" Nate asked dipping a sponge finger into the coffee mix. "Mmm... good!"

"I think I've wrapped up the case. Well, at least the aspects that are related to the fire."

"Still some missing bits?"

"Not really, because Abi's the mystery and there's nothing connecting her to the cause of the fire. She was just unfortunate — her boyfriend died during the night and she left his body to burn in the fire. Well, at least that's the story she's telling. And, according to Beauty, she had to wake Abi up to get her out of the building. So, nothing there."

"What's going to happen to her now?"

I shrugged.

"Luke, the guy that I was trying to get to speak to, finally came in from the Midlands. He's in police custody, and he's been helpful to their investigation. I just had to contact the guys that were looking for him so that the police could pick them up. I think they've got definite links to the fire and they've been blackmailing Luke to push drugs for them. It's only after Luke came in that the detective — Jones — agreed to have the fridges at the shop examined. I'm confident that they'll find something."

"Huh, crazy! So, what was their motive, do you think?"

"Revenge — that Andy guy and his friends got beaten up by Pablo and this other guy who's gone back to India. Seems a bit extreme but there is no other connection. I think they quickly saw that Luke was the weakest link — he needed money. They somehow coerced him into running the county lines."

"County lines — listen to you, Shortie. You sound like a real dic."

"I've enjoyed this much more than my regular nine-to-five. Wish I could do it — you know."

"Wow! I don't know what to say," Nate said, stepping away from the kitchen counter so that he could remove his sweater. He backed away a little further. "Time for a quick shower?" he asked, disappearing into the corridor.

I stared after him wondering why I had made such an effort with dinner. I poured the tiramisu mixture into a large glass over the finger sponges and threw in a few raspberries in between each layer of the other ingredients. I grabbed a spoon and slouched onto the sofa with one of the glasses.

Nate reappeared a few minutes later with the air of mint and green tea shower gel. Noticing the glass in my hand, he slid onto the small area of sofa left beside me. We sat quietly for a bit.

"Maybe if we took things a bit slower."

I spun my head round to check his expression.

"You breaking up with me?"

"Don't be... no, of course not. I mean slow with these changes."

"Well, I didn't say that I was going to start now. I just want to do this in the future. I'm just not looking forward to going back to work full-time, that's all. It just feels a bit stale."

"What about a sabbatical? They'd pay your salary, right? And perhaps you could use the time to learn a bit more, get some proper licences and see if you could get some paying clients. I mean — I don't know anything about the business, but I could help you get set up. We've got a room in the office complex that we aren't using at the moment."

"I'll think about it — I don't think a sabbatical will work, but I'll ask anyway."